SEALED FOREVER

Bone Frog Brotherhood Book 3

SHARON HAMILTON

SHARON HAMILTON'S BOOK LIST

SEAL BROTHERHOOD BOOKS

SEAL BROTHERHOOD SERIES

Accidental SEAL Book 1

Fallen SEAL Legacy Book 2

SEAL Under Covers Book 3

SEAL The Deal Book 4

Cruisin' For A SEAL Book 5

SEAL My Destiny Book 6

SEAL of My Heart Book 7

Fredo's Dream Book 8

SEAL My Love Book 9

SEAL Encounter Prequel to Book 1

SEAL Endeavor Prequel to Book 2

Ultimate SEAL Collection Vol. 1 Books 1-4 /2 Prequels

Ultimate SEAL Collection Vol. 2 Books 5-7

SEAL BROTHERHOOD LEGACY SERIES

Watery Grave Book 1

Honor The Fallen Book 2

Grave Injustice Book 3

BAD BOYS OF SEAL TEAM 3 SERIES

SEAL's Promise Book 1

SEAL My Home Book 2

SEAL's Code Book 3

Big Bad Boys Bundle Books 1-3

BAND OF BACHELORS SERIES

Lucas Book 1

Alex Book 2

Jake Book 3

Jake 2 Book 4

Big Band of Bachelors Bundle

BONE FROG BROTHERHOOD SERIES

New Year's SEAL Dream Book 1

SEALed At The Altar Book 2

SEALed Forever Book 3

SEAL's Rescue Book 4

SEALed Protection Book 5

Bone Frog Brotherhood Superbundle

BONE FROG BACHELOR SERIES

Bone Frog Bachelor Book 0.5

Unleashed Book 1

Restored Book 2

SUNSET SEALS SERIES

SEALed at Sunset Book 1

Second Chance SEAL Book 2

Treasure Island SEAL Book 3

Escape to Sunset Book 4

The House at Sunset Beach Book 5

Second Chance Reunion Book 6

Love's Treasure Book 7

Finding Home Book 8 (releasing summer 2022)

Sunset SEALs Duet #1
Sunset SEALs Duet #2

LOVE VIXEN
Bone Frog Love

SHADOW SEALS
Shadow of the Heart

SILVER SEALS SERIES
SEAL Love's Legacy

SLEEPER SEALS SERIES
Bachelor SEAL

STAND ALONE BOOKS & SERIES
SEAL's Goal: The Beautiful Game
Nashville SEAL: Jameson
True Blue SEALS Zak
Paradise: In Search of Love
Love Me Tender, Love You Hard

NOVELLAS
SEAL You In My Dreams Magnolias and Moonshine

PARANORMALS

GOLDEN VAMPIRES OF TUSCANY SERIES
Honeymoon Bite Book 1
Mortal Bite Book 2

Christmas Bite Book 3

Midnight Bite Book 4

THE GUARDIANS

Heavenly Lover Book 1

Underworld Lover Book 2

Underworld Queen Book 3

Redemption Book 4

FALL FROM GRACE SERIES

Gideon: Heavenly Fall

NOVELLAS

SEAL Of Time Trident Legacy

All of Sharon's books are available on Audible, narrated by the talented J.D. Hart.

ABOUT THE BOOK

At forty years of age, Special Operator Tucker Hudson re-qualifies and joins SEAL Team 3 but must leave behind his young bride. He steps into a dangerous deployment in Central Africa to hunt down a drug and child sex trafficking warlord. But the hazardous duty is made even more perilous by the knowledge that his best friend and team buddy, Brawley Hanks, suffers from effects of his previous deployments.

Brandy Hudson knows her big man with his huge heart must do what he's called to do to protect his team both in the arena and at home. She hopes that his sacrifice will not prove too precious. But she also knows this comes with being the wife of an elite warrior. He's the man she's searched for her whole life.

Their relationship will be tested while they stay connected during his deployment and afterwards. Brandy knows she must brace herself for whatever happens when he comes home.

But life is not always fair as tragedy strikes their SEAL family, and rocks the foundations of their love to the core. Will they be the couple to survive, or will one of them be left behind?

Book 3 of the Bone Frog Brotherhood.

AUTHOR'S NOTE

I always dedicate my SEAL Brotherhood books to the brave men and women who defend our shores and keep us safe. Without their sacrifice, and that of their families—because a warrior's fight always includes his or her family—I wouldn't have the freedom and opportunity to make a living writing these stories. They sometimes pay the ultimate price so we can debate, argue, go have coffee with friends, raise our children and see them have children of their own.

One of my favorite tributes to warriors resides on many memorials, including one I saw honoring the fallen of WWII on an island in the Pacific:

"When you go home
Tell them of us, and say
For your tomorrow,
We gave our today."

These are my stories created out of my own imagination. Anything that is inaccurately portrayed is either my mistake, or done intentionally to disguise something I might have overheard over a beer or in the corner of one of the hangouts along the Coronado Strand.

I support two main charities. Navy SEAL/UDT Museum operates in Ft. Pierce, Florida. Please learn about this wonderful museum, all run by active and former SEALs and their friends and families, and who rely on public support, not that of the U.S. Government. www.navysealmuseum.org

IF YOU GOT ANY CLOSER, YOU WOULD HAVE TO ENLIST

I also support Wounded Warriors, who tirelessly bring together the warrior as well as the family members who are just learning to deal with their soldier's condition and have nowhere to turn. It is a long path to becoming well, but I've seen first-hand what this organization does for its warriors and the families who love them. Please give what your heart tells you is right. If you cannot give, volunteer at one of the many service centers all over the United States. Get involved. Do something meaningful for someone who gave so much of themselves, to families who have paid the price for your freedom. You'll find a family there unlike any other on the planet. www.woundedwarriorproject.org

CHAPTER 1

NAVY SEAL TUCKER Hudson squinted across the beach bonfire that roared taller than any of the men on his SEAL Team 3. He was back—at least in all the ways he could be at forty years of age. A retread. He'd survived the landmines of past deployments and the vacancy of those years off the teams, as well as the grueling BUD/S training re-qualifying for his spot. He was ready for his first mission as a new *silver* SEAL, as the ladies called him. He was a Bone Frog, one of the old guys on SEAL Team 3.

He was ready for the do-over. Told himself he deserved it. But just to add a little gasoline to the fire in his soul, his childhood best friend, Brawley Hanks, was failing. And that's what ate at him.

Brawley had just spent six months in rehab while Tucker completed his SQT, SEAL Qualification Training. His chief, Kyle Lansdowne, had misgivings about allowing Brawley to go on the next mission to

Africa, but since Tucker would be there, his LPO had overruled a suggestion from higher up to sit him out. This didn't help Tucker's nerves any. He knew it was his job to cover all that up and make those jitters disappear.

He watched the ladies dancing around the bonfire and looked for his wife of two months. Brandy cooed over Dorie and Brawley's little pink daughter while Dorie showed her off. The toddler was fast asleep. Several of the Team's kids jumped to get a look at the child until Dorie knelt and let them stand in a circle and check her out.

Their particular SEAL platoon tradition made them gather at the beach before a new deployment. All the wives, the kids, the close girlfriends, and occasionally parents were there. But only those on the inside, in the know. Some had lost loved ones. Some had been injured. Some had suffered too much. But these were the people who held them all together—who would hold Brandy together while he was gone.

The past two years with Brandy had been the hardest but most rewarding years of his life. When he was a younger SEAL, sometimes the ladies made him nervous since he didn't have anyone to come home to. But now that he did, now that he could actually lose something dear to him, it made this little celebration all the more special. He'd missed those evenings under the stars in Coronado, surrounded by life and the promise of living forever.

No one else would understand this kind of SEAL brotherhood, Tucker thought. You had to live it to know how it felt to be part of this family. You had to cry and celebrate with these people, tell them things would turn out, somehow. The miraculous would happen, because it always did. That's who they were. There wasn't any other group in the whole world he'd rather be a part of.

He'd tried doing without before. He knew better.

Tucker studied the beautiful, round face of his new bride and all her other curves that enticingly called to him by firelight. It seemed she grew more and more stunning every day. Her eyes met his, and he glanced down quickly, embarrassed that he might look like a teenage boy. But that's the way he felt. He was back to being the big, quiet kid the Homecoming Queen or head cheerleader came over to tease. It used to happen a lot in high school and he'd never gotten used to it.

Chief Petty Officer Kyle Lansdowne took up a seat next to him. His chief was the most respected man on the team, even more than some of the officers, who were never invited to these events. Kyle had worked hard to make sure Tucker came to his squad. Although slightly younger than Tucker or Brawley, Kyle's experience leading successful campaigns through sticky assignments made him one of Team 3's most valuable assets.

"You nervous?" his LPO asked.

"You asked me that the day of my wedding, remember?"

Kyle nodded.

"I was nervous then." Tucker took a pull on his long-necked beer. "I know what I'm getting into this time." He smiled, which was reflected back to him.

"Well, you know what they say about leading men. Don't ask a question you don't know the answer to first." Kyle clinked his bottle against Tucker's.

"Hey, meant to give you a big congrats on making Chief."

"I have the best fuckin' platoon on the Teams. Makes it easy," Kyle said with a wink.

"Easy? You fuckin' said easy? That's B.S. and you know it."

They clinked glasses again and watched the children fawning over Brawley's daughter, still sleeping by the firelight, tucked in Dorie's arms. Kyle's two were right in the middle of them. Brandy gave Tucker a sexy wave.

"You got a good one, Tucker. I'm really happy for you," Kyle whispered, continuing to follow the ladies.

"You bet I did." Tucker meant every word he uttered. He'd always liked women he could grab onto and squeeze without breaking half her ribs. Brandy had the heart he did and that fierce joy of living, which also matched his own. And she'd earned that because of how she'd fought for every ounce of respect she so richly deserved. She spoke her mind. She loved with abandon, and he was damned lucky to have her in his corner. He was also grateful she let him go off and be a warrior again, just when most friends his age had wives ragging on them to quit.

And that was okay too. The SEAL teams were a revolving door of fresh and old faces, and internal dramas played out every day all over the world. It was sometimes hardest on the families. Men had to consider all of that when they played Varsity.

Kyle searched the crowd.

"I haven't seen him in about twenty minutes," Tucker mumbled. It worried him, too, that Brawley wasn't nearby. "I think he might have gone to get more beer, but that's just a rumor."

He knew Kyle suspected he was making up a safe story, which is why he didn't say a word. Then his chief slowly turned, facing him. "You let me know if he gets shaky, and I thoroughly suspect he will." Kyle's voice was low, avoiding anyone else's ears.

The two men stared at each other for a few long seconds.

"I got it, Kyle. He's not on his own."

"And you only risk a little. Don't let that go over the edge."

"We don't leave men behind." Tucker knew Kyle understood what he meant.

"No, we don't. I want you both upright. Both of you, Tucker."

"Roger that."

They gripped hands. Then Kyle broke it off and punched him in the arm.

"Dayam, Tucker. You can stop drinking those protein shakes anytime now."

Tucker liked that thought but dished some trash talk back. "Lannie, it ain't protein shakes. It's her," he said, aiming his beer bottle at Brandy. "You should see how she works me out."

Kyle stood up and then murmured, "I can't unsee that, dammit," and disappeared into the crowd.

Tucker hoped Brawley would show himself soon. His "ghosting" wasn't a good sign. He should be at Dorie's side. Tucker kept searching and then finally spotted Brawley pissing into the surf, which meant he was drunker than he should be.

Come on, Brawley. You're gonna get us both killed.

Brandy was still occupied with the women, and Kyle was having a little nuzzle time with Christy while carrying one of his two on his shoulders. Tucker scrambled to his feet and strolled toward his best friend, who was now throwing rocks into the ocean. His jeans were wet, and he was barefoot.

Brawley Hanks grew up alongside Tucker's family in Oregon. He couldn't ever remember a time when they weren't best friends. Always competitors when it came to sports and girls, even enlisting in the Navy the same day, they attended the same BUD/S class. They'd planned on getting out after their ten years, but close to the end, Brawley met Dorie, and, well, the poor guy couldn't help himself and got hitched up. She had pushed for the re-signing bonus so they could buy a nice house in Coronado. A beautiful, classy girl with all the wildness Brawley had, Dorie was missing his self-destructive bend.

Tucker wondered at first if their marriage would survive, but as Brawley showed all the signs of getting seriously embroiled in a lusty kind of full-tilt love that made him go stupid and do dumb things like buy flowers, Tucker became convinced his friend had finally been tamed and had given up his wandering ways.

Except that after his last two deployments, Brawley returned to his old ways—being the bad boy he'd always been before he met Dorie. He drank and chased too much. And although they had high hopes for his rehab, Tucker wasn't as convinced as Brandy or Dorie that his bad days were behind him.

"Hit any fish yet?" he asked Brawley.

"Fuck no," Hanks replied, slurring his words and letting go of another smooth, flat stone. It didn't skip like he'd been aiming to do.

"You know the more you hit the ocean, that ocean is gonna get you back, Brawley."

"I'm registering my complaint."

Tucker had to proceed with caution. He was at one of those turning points. But if Brawley lost it, at least he'd lose it here and save Kyle the trouble of having him sent home in shame. It sucked to be thinking this way just a day from deployment, but it was what it was. No sense sugar-coating it.

"I think your registration is going to the wrong department. Got your branches of service mixed up, Brawley. You should take it up with the man upstairs. Have you had that conversation recently?"

Brawley squinted back at him, as if the moonlight hurt his eyes. He did look like a big teenager, albeit a lethal one.

"I wear the Trident. Poseidon and Davy Jones are my buds. The man upstairs has given up on me."

His challenge hit Tucker in his stomach. *You dumb fuck. Where are you goin'?*

He walked to within inches of Brawley's hulking form. Inhaling deeply, he worked to calm himself down so it would be effective. He knew he only could say this once, so he made sure Brawley didn't misunderstand his steely stare.

"I'm going to remind you that you brought a daughter into the world. What kind of a world do you want her to grow up in, you old fart? You want her to grow up with an angry son-of-a-bitch for a father like you did, Brawley?"

His best friend started to interrupt him, and Tucker grabbed his ears and spit out his message.

"Or were you thinkin' you'd check out over there in that shit African red clay, making Dorie a widow and your daughter fatherless? Maybe causing the death of one or more of your friends who have pledged their lives to save your dumb ass. You willing to take us all with you? You want to be that kind of best friend to me, Brawley? Or are you gonna man-up?"

Tucker released Brawley's ears and pivoted like a Color Guard. He thanked his lucky stars he hadn't gotten clobbered with that delivery and called it good. Whatever Brawley did next was up to him.

It was just something that had to be delivered *before* they left for Africa. After they were there, it would be too late.

Tucker had done all he could.

CHAPTER 2

BRANDY HELD LITTLE Jessica, who began to stir and then fuss. She knew the toddler would sense she wasn't in her mother's arms, and it didn't take long. Jessica's blue eyes opened wide and then squinted, as if she considered going into a fearful cry, but then smoothed out as Brandy whispered down to her,

"You know me, Jessica. It's your auntie Brandy. And Mommy is right here, see?" She propped the child at an angle so she could see her mother standing next to Brandy. Dorie gave her another funny face and tickled her under her chin, which made Jessica giggle.

But when the squirming got to be more pronounced, Brandy handed her back to her mother.

"She's getting big. Can't believe how heavy she is now," Brandy said to her best friend.

"I know it. I fear she's going to take after Brawley's side of the family."

Both of them laughed.

"How are they these days?" Brandy asked.

"As weird as ever. Brawley's dad is having some health issues. She's trying to get him to give up drinking."

"Oh, Lord. I thought she was smarter than that."

"Brawley says it was a good talk with his dad, one of the best they'd had recently."

Brandy remembered the day of Dorie and Brawley's wedding. Mr. Hanks was so proud of his son for following in his Team footsteps, even if Brawley hadn't yet made it to twenty years like his father did. She remembered how tender Tucker was about the older man. The story had touched her, how this gruff old guy stood by his often cold and emotionally distant wife and two daughters. He was tough as nails with Brawley, but loved him intensely. She knew old man Hanks lived through Brawley.

She searched the crowd for Tucker and found him returning to the campfire, alone. He struck up a conversation with several newbie SEALs—froglets, as they were called.

Dorie was swinging Jessica around, singing. The firelight on her face melted the lines and dark shades her face had shown of late.

Honeymoon is over. Now the real life begins.

When Dorie took a bench, Brandy sat next to her and they swayed, shoulder to shoulder, like they'd done so many times over the past few years—before they were married, before Dorie's little girl, and before all the trouble that was brewing.

She wanted to ask her friend how things were going but didn't want to intrude or shatter what simple sense of peace the night gathering was giving her. The stars were out now. Someone was playing a guitar and laughter erupted as older children splashed in the evening surf, monitored by hovering moms and dads.

She remembered the 4th of July fireworks at the Santa Cruz Boardwalk her parents took her to once when she was a child. That night, they lay back on the blanket spread for all of them, holding hands, the three of them watching the night sky light up and sparkle as if it would go on without end.

Those were special summer days. Holding on to the hands of the two most important people in her life, inoculated against the screams of the Big Dipper coaster. She was never afraid when they both were there. It never occurred to her that these happy days wouldn't last forever. She made a mental note to enjoy what today, what tonight was and was not—to cherish it. And instead of the steady hands of her parents, she now had her big man with his basketball hands and arms the size of small tree trunks who could hold her tight if ever she was afraid and, in the most delicate of ways, hold her heart in the palm of his enormous hand.

She'd always been a woman to barge ahead and make space for herself, especially since opportunities weren't offered to her as often as they were for beautiful women like Dorie. Brandy had to work for it, yet, in Tucker's arms, she almost felt as fragile and delicate as a small bird.

Jessica had fallen asleep again, so Brandy offered to hold her, giving her mother's arms a break. The cherub leaned against her soft chest and grabbed the folds of her sundress in her sleep. She smelled clean. Her warm breath was soothing. Someday Brandy knew she'd like to hold one of her own, when the right time came along.

She glanced up and caught Tucker watching her rocking Dorie's daughter. His warm smile sent an electric spark down her spine. Her eyes watered as she inhaled and let her heart soak up all the love she had for this man. She was the luckiest girl in the world.

Dorie rested her head on Brandy's shoulder. "Look at that big oaf. He loves you so much. You can just tell the way he looks at you. I've never seen him so happy, Brandy," her best friend said, breathlessly.

"Who knew, right?" Brandy referred to the fact that he'd always been considered a permanent bachelor, just as she had fit the old cliché *"always a brides-maid…"* He was strong as an ox and fiercely loyal but not the womanizing type, and so he had never been chased. That was something else they had in common.

Dorie noticed the tears in her eyes. "It's okay to cry, Hon. What you two have is special." She raised her head and angled it the opposite direction. "Sometimes, I envy you so much."

That was always how Brandy had felt, being Dorie's plus-sized friend, who was good-natured, positive, easy to talk to, but not the stunner Dorie was. She was aware that sometimes men befriended her just to get closer to Dorie.

All that had changed. And now Dorie was filled with envy of the love she shared with Tucker.

"Welcome to my world, Dorie. I used to feel that way about you every time we went somewhere. Then it was you and Brawley, the perfect couple. I wanted that so much."

"And see? You got it."

There was an awkward pause, and she found the courage to ask that question she'd been needing to. "So how's he doing?"

Dorie sat up straight. She pulled her oversized sweatshirt over her knees and wiggled her bare toes in the sand then re-clipped her hair, which she always did when she was thinking. "He's nervous. But I think he'll do all right. He just needs to prove to himself that he can handle the load."

Brandy nodded. "Tucker will keep an eye out for

him. He looks ready," she said and then wished she could take it back.

They grew silent again. "He's got good meds, when he takes them. He'll be on them the rest of his life, the doctor told us. But he still is getting used to how they feel. I know he worries it will affect his reaction times."

"Performance anxiety. He'll shake it off, Dorie. You'll see." She wanted to be as positive as she could. She wanted to believe every word, but deep inside, she had some niggling doubts.

It was time to change the subject.

"You have plans for the two of you when they're overseas?"

"Mom wants me to go on a cruise with her, but I don't want to take Jessica, and I don't want to leave her."

"Let me take her. I'd love to help out. You just let me know. Go have that vacation with your mom," Brandy whispered.

Dorie smirked. "It's not a real vacation being with her, especially when she's between boyfriends. I feel like I'm the chaperone and she's the wayward teenager."

Brandy laughed. "Good point. You and your mom have always been like that, though. Take advantage of it while she's outrageous. I'd give anything to have just one more day with my mom. It's been over sixteen years and I still miss her every day."

Dorie put her arm around her shoulders. "Sweetie, you deserve a big hug for that one. We'll just help each other, then. And you should paint. Your sketches are beautiful, Brandy. Maybe this will give you time to explore that part of yourself you can't when he's around. And it might help you get your mind off worrying about what they're doing and if they're safe."

"I'll need some of that."

"We both will."

TUCKER WAS QUIET on the ride home. Brandy snuggled against him in the front seat, tucking herself under the protection of his huge wing. She could feel his thoughts.

They would have tonight together and all day to-morrow. One last chance for a perfect Sunday, and then it was early to bed for his four o'clock trip to the base for transport overseas. It was the first time she would be home alone knowing Tucker wasn't on a training exercise but an actual mission.

His chest began to rumble. "You're doing really well, honey. It will be over before you know it. The second and third time, they say it gets easier. After that, well, they'll be asking all the newbie wives to hang around you for advice and comfort. You'll see. Christy, Dorie, and the other wives will take good care of you."

"Thanks, Tucker. I'll try to check in with your folks and sister a bit too."

"They'd love that. But don't be surprised if my mom gets you worried. She's the worrier in the Oregon clan. Always was. Even worse now, I think."

"But she's so proud…" Brandy started to say.

"She doesn't favor the odds, the more I go over. It's just a fact of deployment."

Brandy knew it was one thing to be married to the love of her life knowing he was going over to a foreign and very hostile environment and quite another to raise a son going into harm's way.

"I totally get it, Tucker." She withdrew and studied his face. They had parked at her bungalow. "Only thing that makes it okay is that I know it's what you love. Who would I be if I tried to stop you from your desires?"

His grin shone in the moonlight.

"Speaking of those desires…" he mumbled then covered her mouth with his. "I want to make some memories in the next few hours we have left so I'll have things to dream about over in the jungle." His hand brushed her cheek tenderly. "I won't be sad if I focus on the homecoming," he whispered before he claimed her hungry mouth.

Their kisses turned into heavy petting. Her bra became unhooked. His head barely fit under the tight tee shirt until she pulled it up around her neck. He hoisted her up onto his lap after he slid beyond the steering wheel. She slowly pressed her mound over his groin and followed his hard edge then repeated the movement, back and forth, loving the stimulation. She was getting soaked with her own juices.

She framed Tucker's face between her hands. His wet lips and tongue had abused her nipples, which knotted and perked for him. His paw grazed down her rear, seeking entrance to her core with two long, probing fingers. She bent her knees at his hips and rose up just enough so he could feel her heat and the wetness of her desire.

"Baby, I want to do this right here, right now, so if that's what you want, I'm good with it," he whispered.

"Anytime, Tucker. Anywhere."

It was tight in the cab of his truck, but she managed to move down on him, eventually finding and covering his shaft, setting off the horn in only one staccato burst. She didn't even look outside to see if her father, who lived in the big home in front, had heard them.

And she could tell Tucker hadn't even noticed.

CHAPTER 3

TUCKER AWOKE TO the smell of bacon and coffee. Their Sunday routine usually meant sleeping in and staying in bed fooling around as long as possible, often until lunch. But he knew she was making him a memorable breakfast, to add to some of the memorable things they'd done last night in the truck and again in the bed until they both collapsed.

But today, he felt ready to go, ready to do it all over again. And he was starved.

He donned his American flag boxers and padded his way to the kitchen, where Brandy hummed a new country tune they liked. She wore her pink fuzzy robe, the one that was a tad bit small for her, not that he was complaining. The thing gaped open and only managed to keep her back and shoulders warm. It did nothing to cover up her luscious chest or that delicious triangle between her legs he was hoping to explore soon.

She was barefoot, her hair clipped atop her head,

one hand holding a red coffee mug and the other massaging bacon with a red spatula. Brandy's smile could warm the North Pole. He especially liked the bruises she had on the right side of her neck.

"Look at you!" he growled.

She pointed the red spatula at him. "Look at *you*!" she returned. "All dressed up and nowhere to go."

He moved around to her backside while she continued to cook the bacon. He let her feel his hardness as his knees bent slightly, connecting their thighs. "I have something for you. Just take a seat," he said in a raspy whisper before carefully kissing an especially large reddish-purple bruise under her right ear.

"But I got bacon and coffee, Tucker," she murmured.

"I got bacon for you, sugar."

She wiggled her butt against him. His hands were inside her robe and, in one easy move, had turned off the stovetop and hoisted her up in the air, carrying her back to the bedroom.

"I wanted to make you something special," she giggled, still holding the red spatula.

"Oh, you are, honey. I can't wait to taste it."

He tossed her on the bed. She threw the spatula at him.

"So you want to fight? I can fight with you, honey." He pulled her ankles toward him, dropped his drawers, and was nearly inside her swollen lips when his phone rang. The ringtone meant it was Brawley.

"God dammit!"

"Just forget it. Put it in, Tucker."

"I'm going to, but I gotta take this call."

"Fuck me, Tucker. I promise to be real quiet."

He liked her spunk and her compliance, but he crawled over the bed, reaching for the phone at the side table. She was moving her body up to match him, pulling his butt checks down, trying to get him positioned for lovemaking.

"Brawley, your timing sucks," he said to his teammate.

"Oh, that's right. It's your fuck day."

Tucker held the phone out to Brandy while he began to give her another hickey. Brandy laughed.

"Hi, Brawley," she teased. "Go ahead and talk, but Tucker's sort of preoccupied at the moment."

She squealed as Tucker's tongue slid between her legs.

"You guys are both assholes," he squawked through the phone. "Guess I'll go do my PT by myself. No fun running with someone who can't keep up, anyway."

Tucker jerked to attention. "I can keep up. I can whoop your ass any day."

Next, they heard a tap on Brandy's bedroom window and discovered Brawley standing just outside, in the garden, with his cell phone to his ear.

Brandy screamed and dove for the bedcovers. Tucker lifted a pillow to cover himself then disconnected the call.

"Fuckin' jerk. I'll be right out," he shouted. To Brandy, he pulled aside the blankets. "I'm so sorry, sweetheart. Let me get a timed run in, and I'll be right back, if that's okay."

She smiled. "I'll get the breakfast finished and will put the eggs on when you get back. I got biscuits and blackberry jam my dad made last week. You could invite Brawley, if you want."

"No way," he said as he pulled on his running shorts and a tee shirt and then slipped into his running shoes. From the dresser, he retrieved his fitness watch. "I'll be back in about an hour, maybe a little longer. But I have plans for that blackberry jam." He wiggled his eyebrows.

She was still curled in fetal position, her tempting pink body parts peeking out from beneath the covers. "I'll be ready." Coming to her knees, she held up a sheet to cover her frontside and looked up to him with a sexy smile. "Have a good run."

Once outside, Tucker jumped into Brawley's truck, and the two of them took off toward the beach for their five-mile run and swim cool down. Brawley had music on loud, so a conversation was out of the question.

When they parked at the State beach, Tucker took advantage of the near-silence.

"You really are an asshole. Last morning before we leave. Did it ever occur to you I might have had other plans, you jerk?"

"Oh, I knew what you were probably doing or had just finished doing or were getting started doing. Look at it this way, I'm saving you from the excuse that you don't need to work out today. You're an old guy, Tucker. You don't have all the stores the younger ones have."

Brawley said the last bit while running quickly away from Tucker, over the sand dune covered in ice plant, and heading for the firmer sand by the surf.

Tucker had to work to catch up to him, and then Brawley turned on the speed, not giving him an ounce of respite. But Tucker had everything he needed, and the anger in his gut gave him a little more. He never let Brawley lead, not even by a nose.

At the conclusion of their run, they dove into the surf and paddled out into the inlet, doing a buddy swim in tandem. Tucker's swim stroke was the most challenging for him now at his age and weight. Although he'd kept up his timed runs and weight training, finding time for swim workouts had been difficult over the past ten years. His older body preferred a pool over the oily and dank inlet.

He considered trimming down his body size after this next deployment. Brawley was a natural swimmer, and Tucker could barely keep up to him until the last stretch, when he pulled away and left Tucker feeling like he was dogpaddling behind. Emerging from the surf, he found Brawley sunning himself on the sand, waiting. His eyes were closed, covered with the trim dark sunglasses they all wore that hugged his face.

Tucker kicked a little sand onto Brawley's chest.

"Ah, thanks for the catnap, grandpa."

"I'm only a month older than you are. Give me a session at Gunny's Gym and you'll drop that cocky attitude."

Tucker stood slightly taller than Brawley, but both of them were two of the tallest SEALs on Team 3.

Tucker reached down to give a hand, pulling Brawley up.

"You game for a protein shake or coffee?" Brawley asked as both men retrieved their shoes and shirts and then ambled barefoot to the truck.

"Nah, I gotta get back. Brandy's got biscuits and her famous cheesy scramble and some homemade blackberry jam I'm dying to devour. I'm famished."

"Suit yourself."

Brawley covered the front seat with a couple of old beach towels he retrieved from behind the cab. Tucker rubbed the sand from his feet and ankles, dropped his running shoes on the floorboards and positioned his wet lower torso carefully on the fluffy towel.

"You have plans for today?" he asked Brawley.

"Dorie wants to take Jessica to the aquarium, so I think we'll head over there and have a picnic. We had a rough night with the little one up every two hours. When I left, they were both crashed, finally, so I'm going to let them sleep as long as they can."

"Good idea."

"You?"

"Just fooling around. Gotta finish packing, clean my Sig, and double check the rest of my gear. It's not second nature yet, but I know it will be, so I'm doing everything twice. You need anything for your kit in case I stop by the base?"

"I'm good."

They rode in silence until they turned onto the road leading to Brandy's bungalow. Her dad's truck was gone, so Tucker made a note to make a quick stop at the store to say good-bye.

"I meant to talk to you a little over coffee, so let me just get something off my chest, Tucker."

Brawley's arms and hands rested at the top of the steering wheel while he waited for permission to continue. He was focused on Brandy's front door as he pulled to a stop next to Tucker's truck.

"Shoot. I'm all ears, now that I'm fully awake."

Sand was itching Tucker's backside as he angled his body, turning to partially face his teammate.

"I wasn't too proud of my behavior last night, Tuck. Had a real anti-social streak going on, and I should have stopped with the drinking much sooner."

"I wondered why you got so hammered. You're getting to be a mean old drunk, Brawley." It was awkward for Tucker to say this, but he wanted to make sure his friend knew it had been noticed.

"Yeah, Kyle said something too."

"We can't do it all, Brawley. You gotta meet us halfway. Just like boat crew. Everyone has to pull their own weight."

Tucker noticed Brawley flinched at those words.

"You have to exercise better judgment. What if something happens and you have to lead the team?"

Brawley looked away, nodding and staring out the driver side window.

"You brought your meds?"

"I got them packed. Went off them yesterday, because, well, I have trouble—"

Brandy had confided that Brawley had impotence issues sometimes when he regularly took the medication cocktails he was prescribed. He guessed this sacrifice of Brawley's demeanor went to no avail since the angry streak probably played havoc with his ability to be intimate. And Tucker knew it wasn't just about performance. Brawley wasn't that kind of guy.

"You can't do that."

Brawley shot Tucker a glare, winced, and rolled his right shoulder. His lips formed a thin straight line. "I wanted to show Dorie—"

"I know all about it, asshole. We've studied those meds in core school. But it's dangerous. You can't go taking risks."

Tucker wanted to leave the conversation alone until they had more time. But he adjusted his attitude and decided he'd give Brawley as much as he needed.

"Dorie's gonna love you anyway, sport. You know that. If you think about it, don't you figure she'd rather have you settled than hard, you dumb fuck?"

"Yup, you're probably right." Brawley's voice trailed off to some place distant.

"Doesn't make you less of a man. Besides, you can do other things, you know, work on it. Make it a project. Make it fun. I think you just need to get used to this new state. You'll figure it out. Only been about, what, four or six months now? But definitely using too much alcohol is a big mistake. That's on you, Brawley."

"I know. I didn't want to be there. I felt like everyone was watching me, looking for tiny cracks."

"You know that's bullshit, Brawley."

"And you're a terrible liar."

"I don't want to preach, but damned if I'm going to

shut up, either. We get over there, and we'll be busy, and I won't have the time."

Tucker waited several seconds for the heavy words to clear. In the small space they shared in private, he continued in a whisper. "Brawley, the only way you'll get through this is to charge right through it. Who cares? You have a medical condition, like someone having a bum hip or a slightly sprained ankle. We watch out for one another. You make good decisions, Brawley, and people will stop watching you." He faced his childhood friend again. "Only way out is through. Right fuckin' through the middle."

CHAPTER 4

BRANDY HEARD BRAWLEY'S truck arrive and was glad she'd decided to shower and get dressed, since their run had taken longer than Tucker had promised. She knew her husband took the responsibility for Brawley's mental state of mind seriously. She had the rest of the day and evening to launch her first good-bye strategy. It was more important that Tucker see she could handle the separation maturely, like she had done when he went off to Great Lakes, BUD/S, and SQT. It was her job to give Tucker one less thing to worry about while he was on a real mission.

He headed barefoot to her front door, tapping sand from between his toes and on his shoes. He left his shoes on the stoop. Wrapping his arms around her, her big man nuzzled in her ear, and apologized.

"Is everything okay?" she had to ask.

Tucker sighed, scanning her face. He was thinking again—choosing his words carefully. Measuring.

Waiting for something that would be revealed later. At last he gave the expected answer.

"I think so. We all just need to give him time. They had a rough night with the kid."

She felt the pang of disappointment, knowing that at some time in the future perhaps they too would have a day before deployment that wasn't ideal. Kids and other family members caused all sorts of chaos. Things get said. People get sick. There were bills to pay and other stresses on young SEAL families.

And there was never enough time to settle everything before they had to leave again. She'd heard the stories. Had happened to people everyone was surprised at. It could derail Tucker and Brandy too.

That's just the way life works sometimes.

"Why don't you go clean up, and I'll have everything ready when you get out?" She followed it with a kiss and a slap on his butt.

"Roger that. I'm off to the shower."

After breakfast, she threw in another load of clothes for his journey to Africa. She watched him search through his things—zip and unzip the packing sleeves and boxes he had organized, counting items in his medic kit, double-wrapping some articles in bubble wrap or foam wedges, and taping others together. He threw in two large rolls of duct tape, a box of disinfectant wipes, bug repellent, and a box of her lavender-scented dryer sheets.

His duty bag contained his specialized equipment, protection devices, and weapons. It would be carried separately with all the other team gear.

He left his clothing bag open as they headed out to run errands.

"Has anyone told you how long it will be?" she asked.

The traffic was blissfully light for a Sunday. He took a back route, away from the potential of distracted drivers unfamiliar with the little roads. It took longer, but it was worth it, he liked to tell her.

"At least a couple of months. It's something new, so we're not replacing another team who's coming home. A lot depends on what we find when we get there."

She knew this, but it was reassuring to hear him explain it again. It verified there was no camouflaged story, just consistent facts.

"Any last-minute instructions? Like when I'll hear from you, or can call you?"

"Not until we get there, Brandy. My phone will be off most of the time. But you can leave me some sexy messages."

He followed it up with a wink. She was going to miss those little half-smiles and winks.

"We're hoping we'll be able to do some face-to-face calls, but we have to be careful about the electronic footprint, so they'll lay it out for us when we get there. They'll establish a protocol."

He suggested she stay close with the other wives but be careful about repeating gossip or treating speculation as truth.

"Things can get blown out of proportion. We don't want to start any marital discord if we can help it," he added.

She'd never thought about that. "I can see why it's important to stay in touch."

"Yep. Christy will give you a call list, and just like the rest of us do when we're home, she'll tell you who you need to be in contact with on a daily basis. I'm guessing you and Dorie will be in the same grouping since you're already best friends. That way, we don't miss anything. Anyone has trouble with the kids or there is an illness, everyone pitches in. You know, life?"

"Yes, I do."

"You get any calls from overseas you aren't positive are from the Navy or one of our team, you disengage."

"You're kidding. You mean I might get calls from Africa? They'll know I'm alone?"

"It could happen. One of my early deployments, one of the wives actually got a telegram. Someone was asking for money, saying her husband had been captured. You know something like that is bogus, right?"

"Of course."

"It would never go down that way. You'd hear from the Navy if something like that happened."

Brandy noted her heartbeat was racing. "You're making me scared, Tucker."

"Good. If it makes you cautious and prepared, good. Be careful who you talk to. Don't volunteer anything. People will want to ask. You can't tell if it's innocent or not. You report anything suspicious to Christy right away, and she'll know how to handle it."

"Got it."

They approached her father's gourmet fruit and grocery store. Tucker continued.

"There is a plan for every eventuality for the families of deployed just like we have. This isn't a group think or rule by committee. Christy calls the shots, and she's the one who has to know everything that's going on at home that's important. You don't ask anyone else's advice or overrule an instruction she's given."

Brandy made the mental note she'd have to stuff down some of her stubbornness, perhaps dial back some opinions as well.

"As long as they're sending you over there prepared, Tucker."

He turned off the truck and chuckled. "Sweetheart. Let me say this one more time."

He took her hand. "Things *always* get fucked up.

No mission ever goes as planned. We're trained for the unexpected and, hopefully, ways we can adjust to any eventuality. That's what we do. We don't get to come home just because they didn't get us the support we needed. We have to make do."

Her stomach rumbled. Tucker must have seen the fear now resident in her eyes and her heart, pulsing throughout her body.

"One thing you need to know that might reassure you. We're the best trained force out there. And I couldn't have a better platoon leader than Chief Lansdowne. Over a third of these guys I've known for over fifteen years, like Brawley. I did this before. I can do it again. And every one of those guys would take a bullet for me without a moment's hesitation."

She began to shake.

Tucker leaned forward and whispered to her lips as he nibbled between words, softly replacing her worry with new flames of desire. "All you have to do is trust me. Trust that it will all work out. Think about the homecoming every single day and every single night. Feel how good it will be to be back together again, okay, honey?"

He pressed deeper. Then she broke it off, came up for air, wrapped her arms around his neck, and hugged him with everything she had. "Just come back to me."

"Nothing human could keep me away."

CHAPTER 5

T UCKER SHOOK THE hand of Brandy's world-class dad, the man who he could count on to keep Brandy from jumping off the rails. He liked that she had this gentle man to confide in. His wise counsel was something not all the other wives had. And, if the worst should befall him, Steven Cook would be a great help in bringing Brandy safely through to the other side.

He didn't like to think about all these things, but now he had more to live for than in his earlier SEAL Team years, and so he had a lot more to lose. He wanted to make sure he did everything he could to prepare them both for the possibility that he could come home injured or worse. Being prepared, even for bad news, was an important step in the grieving process, and it was every SEAL's job to make sure the families had this.

He remembered the advice he'd given Brawley this

morning.

Only way out is to drive right through the middle.

And that's what he was doing right now, hoping he'd covered all the bases.

Steven Cook had been acting casual, appearing to accept Tucker's upcoming trip, but their handshake took far too long, and when they disengaged, his eyes were watering. Tucker hadn't been paying attention to a thing he was saying because he was reading the man's handshake non-verbally.

"Just like a camping trip when I was in the Scouts, Steve. Mosquito repellant, sunscreen SPF over one thousand, moist towelettes, and extra underwear."

"Geez, didn't know they made sunscreen at one thousand SPF," Cook said.

"They don't. I lied." Tucker gave him a grin and winked at Brandy.

Cook laughed and slapped his arm. "If it was me, I'd do a mosquito dip. Those bloodsuckers are big as birds, I've heard."

"Amen to that. When they have to put bars on the holes in the latrines, you know there are some creepy things that can come up and get you. I'm gonna have to get used to spraying my butt with repellent."

Even Brandy laughed at that one. "I thought they have trailers, like shipping containers outfitted with bathrooms and kitchens."

"Yeah, DIY tiny homes," added Cook.

Tucker could only wish. "You remember what I told you about being prepared? If I'm visualizing using a hole in the ground and I got a nice air-conditioned trailer with air freshener, the mental adjustment is not as difficult as the other way around."

"Tucker, I admire how many details you have to pay attention to. Most you guys could run large corporations with the experience you've gained. And you work together as one unit, bringing the best and brightest to places in the world that sorely need it."

"Well, sir, that's why I've never wanted to go to OCS. It's really more like running a zoo, in my opinion. And it's never bothered me to take direction or orders, either, as long as I respect my superiors."

"We ought to make Congress go through your training, Tucker."

"Roger that. Love 'em, but they got one speed and one solution to everything."

"What's that?" Brandy asked.

"Plaster it with paperwork—so much paperwork that no one can move."

The three of them had a good laugh at the expense of some of the men and women who were sending Tucker on his mission tomorrow.

Brandy left to grab water from her dad's walk-in cooler, so Tucker took the opportunity to be frank with her father.

"Steve, you be close to her. She's not going to hear from me as much as she wants. That's going to worry her."

Cook nodded.

Tucker continued. "I think she'll be fine, but you know her. She'll also try to cover it up. Don't let her do that. She can't retreat. She has to stay engaged, connected, even if it means doing busy things to distract from the inherent dangers of warfare. Get her to paint, take a class, or help out more here. Make sure she fills up her days with things so she's not alone."

"She loves to read. I'm sure she'll get a lot of that done."

"Her romances will provide good diversion. I'm totally okay with her reading those." He felt his own cheeks blush at some of the things Brandy had read in her books, adding to her sexual education. He considered himself a very lucky man.

"Tucker, what are you guys doing over there?" Cook asked him.

"Can't say, Steve. The very poor and the very powerful with guns and money make for a deadly combination. Somehow, we're supposed to get between them without getting ourselves killed. Beyond that, we might see no action, or it might be pure hell."

"I'm so happy you're part of our family, Tuck. My

daughter—well, I've never seen her so happy. You be sure to take care."

"Best is yet to come, sir," Tucker said, with a wink.

They said their good-byes. Brandy squeezed her father tight.

"Whoa, wait a minute. You're staying *here*. With *me!*" Cook said, unpeeling her arms from around his neck.

"I just felt like it. That's all," was her response.

They carted the two bags of groceries into the cooler in Tucker's king cab. He'd asked her if she wanted to grab something at the ocean in lieu of a big dinner she'd have to prepare, and she agreed.

Multi-million-dollar yachts, charter ships, and sleek sailing vessels spread out all along the waterway leading to the ocean. Over half of the berths were empty but would be occupied come sunset. They took a table overlooking the water and ordered clam chowder with bread. The warm, creamed soup was soothing on Tucker's stomach as he watched the afternoon sun dance in Brandy's red and mahogany curls, making her appear her head was on fire.

He let his mind wander. He didn't want to overwhelm her this first time with too many instructions. But when he came back, he wanted to sit down and lay down some plans, some future goals, like buying a house, saving their money, and missions they could accomplish together. He was starting late in life to be a new husband. He didn't want to waste any time, but he also didn't want her to feel pressure. He had to take it one step at a time, check this first mission off the list.

So tonight would be about him showing her how much he loved her. How much he was going to miss her. He wanted to thank her for letting him do this gig. He knew he was lucky to have a woman who loved him for what he was and what he wanted to do. Tucker was going to make sure she experienced his love every single day of her life.

He covered her hand with his. "You ready to go?"

When she turned her head and her face was bathed in sunlight again, he discovered she'd been tearing up.

"Honest answer? No. I promised myself I'd be brave."

"You are brave. You're incredibly brave, Brandy. Don't be afraid to show it. It's part of who you are and why I love you so."

He drew her hand to his lips. Their fingers wove together and gently dropped to the shiny shellacked surface of the table. He rubbed her fourth finger with the undersized wedding ring on it he was going to replace as soon as they could afford it, despite what Brandy said.

"Promise me you'll paint. Spend time in the garden and with Dorie and Jessica and your dad, okay?"

"I promise. Can you promise me something too?"

"Sure. What?"

"Write me some letters, Tucker."

"No, ma'am. I'm not a writer."

"I don't care if you think you're a writer. Write what's going on. Just tell me like we were here and you were describing your day. I mean, say the things you can say. Leave out all the—"

He knew what she meant but answered her with humor. "Leave out the bugs, sunburns, flat tires, and snakes, right?"

"Especially the snakes."

"Come on, princess. Let's get you home. I need to add a few things to my bags, and then I'd like to turn in early, if you don't mind."

SHE WASN'T LOOKING at him as she slipped his freshly laundered and folded red, white, and blue boxers into his bag. Her nimble fingers combed over his things like she was looking at them for the last time. Her breathing was a little ragged. She bit her lower lip and he could see the top of her chest was blotchy. Tonight, he'd be gentle with her, kiss every tear away and make her purr like a kitten. He was overwhelmed by her grace, the dignity with which she handled her fear, and the trust she had in him.

He set his phone alarm and then took her by the hand into the shower. As the warm water relaxed them, he kissed her neck and down her spine, rubbing the lemon shower gel over her backside, and then drew his fingers up the front side of her luscious body. When her head rolled back to rest on his shoulder, she moaned.

"Don't ever doubt that I'll return, Brandy," he said as he drew his tongue up and under her ear. He splashed the lukewarm water over her shoulder and smoothed his palm down her front, squeezing the fullness of her breasts, capturing her nipples between his thumb and first two fingers, pinching her.

Her eyes flew open. She turned around, facing him. Arched on tiptoes, she mated her mouth to his, while water cleansed them both.

"And I'll be here, Tucker. I'll always be here," she whispered back to him.

He handed her the fluffy towel scented with lavender. "I can hardly wait."

That brought a smile to her face, finally.

The room turned darker as they slipped into bed. Everything he wanted to tell her, he could do with his touch. He tasted her soft skin, savored the many textures of her body, and explored her dark and sensitive places with his probing fingers. He'd been noticing her effort not to cry, so he did everything in slow motion until he felt hot tears of his own.

As he filled her and held her shattering body in his arms, he wished for a fleeting moment he'd never signed up to leave her. Why had he agreed to risk something so precious he'd waited for his whole life? Why did he ask her to endure that as well? Was it sweeter this way, as he played her body, because he knew now life was so fragile? It all could be over in an instant. Would she ever forgive him if he was the one not coming back—something just an hour ago he was certain could never, ever happen?

Forgive me, Brandy.

After their bodies had cooled, they stared into each other's eyes. His thumb caressed her smooth forehead, and he wiped away the silent tears that streamed down her cheeks into the pillow. Somewhere in the distance, a sea bird was calling. A freight train blew its whistle, and car lights flashed by from the hills looking over the valley floor, quickly dimmed by the consuming darkness of their last night together. It was the eve of his first deployment as a married man. He was whole, complete, content. No matter what, wherever Brandy was, it was home.

Life continues. Everything moves to the rhythm of our hearts. Nothing stops. Nothing stays the same. I am yours forever, Brandy.

He knew now that he could write those letters and exactly what he would tell her.

Tucker was off before dawn, slipping quietly out before Brandy awoke, which was planned. All their good-byes had been done last night, softened with kisses and watered with her tears. To the end, she was strong.

The transport made a stopover in Norfolk for fuel. Once the team landed in North Africa, they took commercial flights to Benin, all of them operated by French and African charter flights used by private contractors and various U.S.-backed aid services. In this way, the team was split up, and arrived from different destinations, in case anyone was watching. Everyone posed as energy consultants working to improve the quality of the electrical grid in Benin.

Tucker's plane was the first to arrive. He and Brawley spent a whole day waiting for the team to assemble and helping to coordinate supplies they'd need for the overland convoy into Nigeria. He found the port village along the coast of Benin fascinating. Its history of the Slave Coast trade had brought tribal leaders much wealth in past centuries, but at a huge price for its people who were caught between waring factions.

The buildings reflected Portuguese and Spanish influences, which gave way to French architecture during the colonial period of the eighteenth to early twentieth centuries. France gave Benin independence in 1950 and, after a couple of decades of Marxist flirtation, was a now a country with a duly-elected administration, sorely in need of foreign aid to keep the peace. The popular vote wasn't always peaceful. The most dangerous times were during elections, but Benin had proved to be a good neighbor to the U.S. and, with help from French intelligence, was deemed a safe landing spot and good cover.

The Team was put up in a tourist hotel overlooking the ocean, that catered to international businessmen. He roomed with Brawley. Kyle had arrived the day before and was off to visit with their French intelligence contact, as well as pick up the vehicles they'd rented. His LPO group took up the top floor of the hotel, but the iron balconies cascaded on the outside like a web of ivy vines. If they wanted to avoid the rickety elevator that was said to work intermittently or the stairs, they could always scale the building with ease. The rest of the team was scattered throughout the hotel.

Brawley was excited to discover an espresso machine in the lobby he didn't have to pay for. It wasn't long before they were talking politics, but they stopped just before they descended into the depths of hell— religion. Tucker knew he'd have trouble sleeping tonight with all the caffeine he'd ingested.

Former professional goalkeeper, Patrick Harrington, and his roommate, Jameson Daniels, had the room next door. The four teammates explored the city together. Patrick dubbed Porto-Novo the "African Riviera" with its old waterfront hotels and large residences of glory days gone by.

"Except a hellofa lot more dangerous. And that's a shame." Tucker knew that in today's world, the port city was far from safe.

"Not safe at the Riviera anymore, either," quipped

Patrick. He'd lived and played throughout Europe during his professional days.

"I get you."

The four bought small trinkets from several tourist shops, including some local refined and scented shea butter, one of Benin's largest exports. They also wandered through a large open-air market that sold produce, fish, palm oil and other items, stocking up on assortments of nuts and dried fruits, including some incredible dates and figs.

Ships of varying sizes docked haphazardly along the waterfront. Most of the boats were for local fisherman and charter crews, but occasionally, there would be a huge yacht guarded by several men bearing semi-automatic weapons. Most the larger crafts were anchored farther out and used jitneys for travel to the town, which Tucker thought would be safer.

The odor of fish mixed with diesel fuel permeated the air, and at times, it was thick with black smoke. Narrow alleys snaked from the main coastal road up the ridge to clusters of colorful, metal-roofed shacks that fanned out in all directions, which appeared to be homes for workers employed in the town. While French was the language Tucker recognized the most, many African dialects that had adapted words from various languages he could recognize. "Cell phone" and "text me" were words he heard quite commonly.

Tiny coffee houses and bars were squeezed between

larger stores and warehouses. A good number of the buildings were abandoned or in the process of being torn down and rebuilt. People were living under blue and green plastic tarps amongst the rubble. In addition to flocks of bicycles, human pushcarts and scooters were the most common forms of transportation.

The four teammates slipped inside a darkly lit coffee house to sit and observe and speak amongst themselves in private.

A barefoot waiter served them thick black coffee poured from a tall Samovar in the middle of their table. It poured like pancake syrup and was accompanied by a chipped bowl of sugar and shea butter chunks light brown in color. When Tucker dropped one into his small cup, it created a creamy foam on top.

"Amazing," gasped Brawley. "I'm taking mine straight."

"Wow!" said Jameson. "A couple of cups of this and my teeth will be permanently stained shit-brown." He smiled, and Tucker could see he was right.

"Not too bad yet, but your breath is foul," answered his roommate, Patrick. He glanced around and studied the two men smoking at the bar. "We got two military-aged males keeping an eye on us over behind you, Tucker."

"Hey, thanks. We all need to keep watch for causing too much interest. Because of where we're from and our accents, they'll be curious what we're doing here," answered Tucker.

"How many deployments did you do in Africa, Tuck?" asked Jameson.

"Not here. We don't use any specialized terms in public, okay?"

"Gotcha."

"But hell yes, I've been to the east coast several times. Mostly I went to the sandbox."

Brawley spoke up. "Kyle and several of the guys spent time off the coast, Cape Verde. Even took a cruise that was a bit exciting."

Tucker had heard all about those trips and about how they had to sneak the ambassador's body home in a food cart aboard another cruise ship.

"Our last trip next door was quite interesting," said Patrick. "I played on the League with fellow from Nigeria who had to flee as a child. This waterfront living is all different, really is like an African Riviera. Inland, it's a whole different place."

"Kind of reminds me of the Caribbean," said Brawley.

"That's a result of the slave trade. How the islands got populated." Tuck finished off his syrupy mixture and then leaned into the table. "This is where Voodoo comes from."

"You've got to be kidding me," mumbled Jameson.

"It was brought to the Caribbean and then New Orleans with the slave traders. The French, who were expelled from Haiti a couple hundred years ago, settled in New Orleans with their French-speaking slaves, and many of the slaves brought their religion with them."

"You've done your research, Tucker."

"I love history. Just read up a bit about Benin. Nigeria was settled by the Brits, but there's lots of crossover. We're supposed to know something about the country we're helping, right?" He grinned and could see he'd impressed the younger SEALs. "When you're home, read up on these places so you'll be prepared. Helps to know who we're dealing with."

Jameson and Patrick nodded. Brawley punched him in the arm.

"If you gents are done, I'd like to move on. Not a good idea to stay too long in one spot if you don't know the neighborhood," Tucker advised.

"Sounds good to me," mumbled Brawley, who was halfway out the door.

Tucker looked for shops that might cater to European contractors and found one fairly large hardware store that sold maps, camping gear, auto parts, and heavy clothing suitable for hiking and fishing. He bought a map of the port, as well as one for the entire country of Benin, and one for Nigeria.

Jameson and Brawley looked over the fishing

equipment, which was sparse. Some of the rods were used.

"That's a good idea," Tucker said. "That would make a good prop to walk around with," he said pointing down at the bucket of rods in varying stages of disrepair.

Brawley bought a small hand-held net, some sisal string, and a small roll of wire. He said he liked the feel of the hunting knife in his hand, so purchased that as well.

Walking back to their rooms at the Hotel Classique, Tucker noticed they didn't draw as much attention as they had before.

Kyle, Cooper, Armando, and Fredo were waiting for them when they returned and were headed out to the airport to pick up the remaining members of their SEAL Team 3 platoon. Much of their specialized equipment was arriving with the balance of the team.

His LPO indicated they would be staying another two days, so Tucker set to re-packing his suitcase. He took a shower, washed out his clothes, and hung them up next to Brawley's laundry. When he reached for his patriotic boxers, something fell out onto the floor. It was a green leather journal slightly larger than the size of his hand. He opened the first page to read her inscription:

Tucker, my love.

I hope you find this easier to chronicle your journey and hope it helps fill the hours until you can return home. My heart is with you, as always. I know the men with you are lucky to have your experience and emotional strength. Enjoy what you can of the trip, and we'll bury or blow up all the other stuff when you get home.

All my love,
Brandy

He chuckled, which drew Brawley's attention. As he fingered through several sketches Brandy had made sporadically throughout the journal in watercolor pencil, his buddy had some choice remarks.

"I'm not checking my bag too closely. I might have gotten a dirty diaper."

"So that's what smells," said Tucker. "Make sure you bring her something nice, Brawley. I think she'd love getting some nice warm Moroccan oil you can drizzle all over her body. It might be the miracle you're searching for."

He hoped Brawley would take it casually, but he wasn't sure. Brawley didn't speak to him the rest of the evening.

CHAPTER 6

TWO DAYS AFTER Tucker left for Africa, Brandy resumed work at her dad's store. She began training the new bookkeeper they'd hired. The little office had recently undergone a DIY makeover with a professional organizer Brandy found. It had been difficult to get anyone to even interview for the job, but after the decluttering and straightening, the space had been turned into a very efficient and sunny little office. No longer were boxes of invoices and books stacked to the ceiling, obscuring the window. She'd purchased attractive curtains and replaced the old AM radio with a new internet receiver and speakers installed around the store so they could stream upbeat music.

One of the things that didn't change was a metal bar of hooks behind the office door her mother had found at an antique store and attached herself. They were sacred, and they were like hands reaching out to hold hers and her father's green aprons. She nixed getting the door painted because it meant the hooks would have to be removed and then replaced. No one was going to do that to her mother's handicraft. She knew her dad would agree without even asking him.

Steve Cook arrived late, nearly Noon. He was wearing a long-sleeved, pinstriped white shirt and green bow tie. He noted her expression.

"Thought I'd start looking the part. I'm the green grocer now."

"The *gourmet* grocer, Dad." She hugged him. "How did you get the nerve to buy that bow tie?"

"I had a few things in my drawers I've not worn for years. I went through some stuff and got rid of tons of old clothes. Ratty with holes or things I was tired of. Decided to splurge on five new shirts, some jeans that weren't so baggy, and two bow ties. You like?"

"Definitely a good look for you."

Brandy had noticed he'd been losing weight, and he'd been using a belt with his faded blue jeans, cinching them up. Today, he looked ten years younger.

Studying his face, she also noticed he'd gotten a haircut and was allowing a bit of salt and pepper stubble to form on his cheeks and chin.

"I like this look, Dad."

He swung the green apron over his head, tied it behind his waist, and spread his arms to his sides.

"Showtime!"

Brandy watched him wander out onto the floor with a new spring in his step. He spoke to several customers before he started ringing in sales.

He was absolutely charming.

She wondered how long this change had been coming, realizing she'd been so preoccupied with Tucker's deployment that she hadn't been focusing on anything else.

As the day turned into late afternoon and early evening, she stopped checking her cell to see if there was a message that Tucker had arrived safely. He'd told her he could only call after their situation was settled and warned her it might take a week to get that established. But it was force of habit, and now she understood it was one more routine she'd have to learn to live without temporarily.

She'd made plans to have dinner with Dorie tonight and headed there after work. Before her best friend could open the door, Brandy heard Jessica's wailing.

"She's gotten hold of a red pen and marked all over our white leather furniture in the living room. Thank God Brawley is gone," said Dorie as she held the squirming child.

Jessica's arms were covered with long lines of red, and several also appeared on her cheeks. As soon as she was set down, the toddler began running full tilt.

Brandy was worried she'd hit a wall and hurt herself. Her shrieking was ear-piercing. Brandy's words of sympathy were completely drowned out.

"Can't leave her unsupervised for a second. This all happened while I was in the bathroom, for Chrissakes," said Dorie breathlessly.

Brandy helped box Jessica off so her mother could pick her up. The toddler immediately wiggled and tried to pry herself loose.

"I don't even know what to use to get this off. It's permanent marker," said Dorie.

Brandy looked at the white couch Jessica had customized. "I'm not sure that will come out. But it will eventually wear off of her. Go put her in the tub. If you have nail polish remover, I can try that on the furniture."

"Oh, I'm not going to bother. I'll just get some slipcovers." Dorie brought the screaming toddler to the bathroom and drew the bath water, disrobing her.

Brandy watched as Jessica stomped her feet and tried every way she could not to cooperate. She fought Dorie as her mother tried to remove her clothes. Even after being placed in the tub, she splashed water and kicked her feet in protest.

"Is she like this all the time?" Brandy asked.

"No. She just gets stubborn. And she has so much energy, Brandy. I blame it on Brawley's side of the family. She's just like him. Her switch is either on or off. Doesn't do anything half-way."

Brandy leaned over the tub and made funny faces. "Jessica, what's gotten into you, sweetheart? You're supposed to *help* your mama now. Don't you want to be a good girl?"

Jessica pounded the water with a resounding, "No!" which made Brandy laugh.

"Just wait, Brandy. You'll see."

"I've been to a few gatherings. Dorie, hate to say it, but a lot of SEAL kids are that way. Tucker calls them little action figures in diapers. I'm sure you've heard the stories too."

"Unfortunately, yes. I'm hoping it's just a phase. And I think kids can sense stress."

Brandy thought the same.

They got Jessica into her sleeper and set her up in a high chair in the kitchen while the two friends prepared dinner. Dorie poured some red wine as they ate their pasta and salad, sharing some of the plain pasta with Jessica.

Having a conversation was impossible as every sentence was truncated and interrupted by Jessica's demands. But as they finished, the toddler got tired and went down to sleep without further incident.

"At last!" said Dorie when she came back to the living room.

"Hope you didn't mind. Borrowed one of your brown towels to sit on."

"No worries."

Brandy didn't want to intrude on their personal life so asked a safe question. "Did you get the call from Christy?"

"Yes, I did. Already got a call from Luci Begay too. Did you know they have a couple of Navajo boys on the mission?"

"No."

"Danny's a peach. Met him at some parties in the past. Danny's cousin, Wilson, is with our guys. He's a SWCC boat guy. Their families are from Arizona, the Navajo reservation."

"Swick?" Brandy hadn't heard the term.

"Those are the guys they use for quick extraction or insertion by water. Wilson's new to the team, but Danny's been with Kyle and Brawley now for over four years."

"I'll make some calls when I get back. That's nice. So they live on the reservation there?"

"Used to. She was a teacher. Works part time now for a charter school here in San Diego. They have two kids."

"I'm guessing she'll be great help to you with Jessica. Wish I could be better support, Dorie."

"Don't be ridiculous. You're my best friend." She

took another sip of wine. "Did you know they're related to one of the original Code Talkers? Their grandfather, I think. A real war hero."

"No, didn't know that. Don't think Tucker's met them yet."

"You learn lots of things. These guys, and sometimes their wives, come from all over. We had a gal from Germany married to one of the SEALs who got injured last time out. Man, did that woman like to go partying!"

"Do we get together as a group?"

"Christy is going to arrange something. When I first started dating Brawley, we all went out shooting! And we'll set up a babysitting pool so we kind of share the load. You don't have to participate unless you want to. She's talking about things like Karaoke too."

"Oh man. Rule me out. I can't carry a tune."

"Safety in numbers, Brandy," she said, holding out her wine glass. "No one can hear any one person when you do it in a group."

"I want to learn all I can. I want to do everything you do. But singing? That's not my thing."

"We got ourselves our very own Cowboy SEAL—Jameson. Used to be a country western star in Nashville. You'll love him. He likes teaching the older kids how to play guitar too."

After a long pause, Dorie asked her how the good-bye went.

Brandy decided to face it head-on. "Broke my heart. I vowed I wasn't going to cry, but I did. Just not made that way. He was so nice. He's been through it before, you know."

"Yeah. Shayla. I never liked her."

"How did you meet?" A ripple of concern crossed her mind. Tucker had told her he'd been divorced over ten years. Had she come back to see him? Her earlier fears returned concerning Brawley's wandering behavior rubbing off on Tucker, though he'd denied it. She was sure she could trust him.

"Shayla came to one of the parties with one of the newbies about three years ago. Even tried to put a spell on Brawley, but he was wary of her. I don't think he ever forgave her for what she did to Tucker."

The information soothed Brandy's nerves but only slightly.

"She likes them young. I think she's a gold-digger. I don't think she stays with anyone very long. Tucker was fortunate he got out in time."

"Well, hopefully, he doesn't compare me too much to Shayla. He was so attentive. Very sweet."

"You're nothing like Shayla. I'm glad."

Dorie poured them more wine and then continued.

"We didn't get that nice, loving send-off. And that happens sometimes. Last time, I was big as a house and very uncomfortable. This time, Jessica wouldn't leave him alone. Almost like she knew he was leaving. Every two hours, it was something. We brought her into bed with us in the end, but neither one of us got much sleep."

"The boys probably got caught up on the plane," said Brandy.

"Hope so. They get pretty keyed up, though. They usually sleep when they get home. I've heard that a lot from other wives. Makes it hard on them sometimes when they need to catch up and crash, but everyone wants them. Just part of what causes the stress of being on the teams, I think."

"Tucker said Brawley looked good. He's expecting him to do fine."

"No comment."

"Dorie, he'll be fine. You gotta believe that."

"No offense, but you haven't walked in my shoes, Brandy. I was worried he wouldn't make it out of rehab." She sighed. "I'm waiting. Just waiting. I've done all I can. Now, it's up to him."

A cold chill descended on the room. Brandy was frightened for the first time in months. Perhaps she hadn't fully understood everything she was getting into. So much could happen to them and to the families at home. Brandy had been confident she had what it took. Yet Dorie had been one of the strongest women she knew and now was struggling.

The talk of Tucker's ex made her feel uneasy. He'd shared his intimate life with someone else, and that someone else could pop back into the brotherhood unexpectantly. She shouldn't feel jealousy, but that's what it was.

Maybe she should have asked more questions. Maybe Tucker had shielded her from some realities that would have made a difference in her decision. Because, if this could affect Dorie and Brawley, it could affect her relationship with Tucker too.

She didn't want to have the worries and thoughts she was having right now. She would have to deal with this because it would eat her alive.

Somehow, she'd have to find the answer.

CHAPTER 7

"LISTEN UP, GANG," Kyle began. "We got a couple new members, so I'm going to make examples of them and give them a bit of shit, if you don't mind."

The group was assembled in the large suite Kyle shared with three others of his senior staff. Three platters of local foods and fruits had been spread out on the dining table, which they devoured in mere minutes. A pallet of bottled water sat on the floor nearby.

"First off, we got SO Tucker Hudson, trained medic, one of our boys from ten years ago. This is his first trip back, and I'm damned glad I could pick him back up. He put in ten as combat medic, and a hell of a good one, too. Now we're going for another ten."

Tucker was embarrassed at the hooyahs and water toasts.

"I intend to get even for those who I didn't catch the last time," Tucker barked. "I know who you are, so be ready," he said, aiming at Fredo, Cooper, Armando, Brawley, and Kyle.

"He rooms with Brawley, so take your complaints up with him," added Kyle.

The team chuckled.

"Okay, now we got some real newbies. DeWayne Huggles is a language specialist, spent a year at school in Monterey, and knows about ten African dialects. He'll help with some of our communications. His French is real sexy too."

A quiet, lanky black kid stood up and gave a shy wave. "I still can't get rid of my Mississippi accent in spite of all the training, but it's a real honor to be part of ya'll's team."

The group greeted him as warmly as they had Tucker.

"He rooms with Ollie," added Kyle. "Next, we got our two SWCC boat crew guys, itching to get you guys transported, if we go that way. Carson Philo here is from California, and he's been deployed with SEAL Team 5 several times and came highly recommended."

Carson gave the hang loose signal without standing up and didn't say a word.

"His roommate is Wilson Nez, who just happens to be Danny Begay's cousin, so don't fuck with him or you'll get a knife between your shoulder blades."

Tucker recognized his Dine features and shook

Wilson's hand since they sat next to each other. Wilson got a proper greeting as well from the group.

"And, Wilson, you're in charge of the porn. That's a newbie thing."

Tucker could see the young boat crew guy was blushing. He'd forgotten that it was the job of the most junior member to haul the trunk with all the dirty magazines and CDs, in addition to their own gear. The crowd shouted "Hooyah!", putting him further in the spotlight.

"This isn't the Scouts, so we don't go around a circle and introduce ourselves and reveal our hobbies. So you get to know your brothers and their specialty on your own. We got the good to go this afternoon from the Headshed, so tomorrow at O-Eight hundred we convoy out, crossing the border into our base camp in Nigeria."

Kyle unrolled a map of both Benin and Nigeria and secured it with tape on the wall. "Our cover is that we're working for international aid—the French, in this case. The contractor is Areva Afrique, a mythical company based out of Paris with offices in Benin. You'll see the logos on our trucks. We'll be working on assessing and strengthening the electrical grid here in both countries, part of the aid package coming from the U.S. and Europe. We'll also help with some humanitarian aid distribution. Some of you medics will be working with the African Doctors' Corps at their various clinics along the way. Some of them are part of our intelligence network."

"Our French liaison is Jean Douchet, a former French Special Forces guy who grew up in Benin and knows many of the tribal leaders here and in Nigeria as well. He also knows those others that we need to stay away from too. He'll be by in the morning to hitch a ride with us. He has a highly skilled and specialized security crew with him at all times."

"Where is our gear, Kyle?" asked T.J. Talbot.

"Got it locked and loaded in the trucks, stored in the parking garage below. Jean has a couple of his private security detail guarding things to make sure they stay that way. We inventoried everything yesterday, and we're looking good."

Tucker was more than ready to start moving. It made him nervous if he had to sit in one place too long. He'd learned from previous deployments it increased the odds of being noticed by the bad guys.

"One other thing about using your cell phones. As I told all of you, we can't use them until we get to the compound. Good news is that we can make video calls by computer there, so some of you can touch base with your families. We'll keep those calls short and then have signups after that when everyone is back in camp. Very important you follow that protocol, so we don't get traced by hostiles.

"In case you didn't notice, you don't exactly fit in as locals, so everyone will be watched. We got lots of nationalities, races, and cultures. Most of the population is Roman Catholic, but those Baptists and Anglicans have been working missions all over the place here and have established mission schools. We got some stubborn Dutch, French, and Brits descended from old families during the colonial period. Even got a few Portuguese and Brazilians, if you can believe it. Jean says they can't always be trusted, so don't. Be cordial, but just be aware. Not everyone who looks American or European can be trusted, okay? You're fair game for petty theft if you're not from here. Some people don't consider it a crime, including some of the police."

Kyle scanned the group, grabbed another water bottle, and continued. "Stay hydrated."

Laughter broke out.

"Okay for the bad news," Kyle said, lowering his voice. The room fell completely silent. "I know some of you won't like this, but we're going to work together here. We may send some of you home earlier than others. We may switch off. But we're probably going to maintain a presence here for a bit, unless something changes, and it always changes."

Tucker heard sighs. Everyone knew not to ask

questions at this point. He just hoped he would be one of the ones to come home early.

"On the coastal region, the bad guys are mostly smugglers, and we're here to learn about their human trafficking. There aren't as many religious zealots as there are in Central and Eastern Africa. Our bad dudes are your garden variety basic criminals dealing in human flesh, and they're very dangerous. Local corruption is rampant, especially among the police. The military here are loyal to their particular jurisdiction, and they're well-trained—some of them even by us, but many by French and Brit teams—so watch out for them."

Kyle continued. "We got African Union troops that will stay out of your way. A lot of U.N. aid goes to training and maintaining those peacekeepers, with some limited success. We got Chinese and Russians trying to curry favor with the traders, as well as the duly-elected politicians who make side deals benefitting themselves and their families. They also interfere with our humanitarian distribution, sometimes steering it toward the smugglers. The Chinese especially would like to get involved in setting up infrastructure partnerships in Nigeria in exchange for oil. There's talk about a huge Chinese port going in next door sometime in the near future. We'd like to find out more about that, too, if we can. As you can see, we got minestrone."

Several people chuckled, and it seemed to ease the tension.

"Drugs aren't as lucrative as the human sex trafficking. They go after mainly young girls, but lately, we've heard young children and older women have gone missing from several villages in the interior. Many of these bands also work out of the Congo or DRC to the south, as well as places farther north. These mini militia groups of bad guys hold up the highways and then sell their pirated goods closer to the ships docked at Porto-Novo and other places along the Nigerian coast. They use the rugged interior jungle region as cover for all their camps and operations, and they're extremely mobile. There's also some gun running going on."

"Make sure you don't look like anything but engineers and electrical contractors or medics. You will be allowed to wear your sidearms starting tomorrow, but keep them hidden and don't take them out unless you're gonna kill someone. Wearing a weapon is commonplace in this part of the world. Even the priests know how to shoot."

He turned to speak to Wilson and Carson. "You two are going to take a team upriver once we get to Nigeria, to explore a couple sites we're curious about. I'm gonna let Jean fill you in on that. We want to get those boats in the water ASAP and make sure everything is set for an emergency extraction should we need it. We need to check out the viability of a water operation."

The boat guys nodded.

"Questions?" Kyle asked.

"We working with any other U.S. operatives or CIA?" Trace Bennett asked.

"Not as of yet. That could change. I'll be in daily contact with State, as well as our ambassadors, as needed. They know we're here, and they've got their ears to the ground. It's very important to both State and our partners that we not escalate the tensions already existing. We get in, get the information about the operation, and then wait for further instructions. It would be great if we could get back to the U.S. without having to fire a shot. That's the goal. But as all of you know, these things change. And we'd like to make it so a few guys can stay behind to continue to collect information on the sex traffickers."

"Are we slated to do hostage rescue?" asked Lucas.

"Not at this time. But again, I wouldn't be surprised if this changes. A lot of these operations are under a cloud. If there is danger to any of our local assets, we might have to act. We're not at war. We're here to back up the people who are trying to negotiate and broker some relief and peace. Those guys are not soldiers. We're the good guys, as you know. We want to make sure we leave it that way when we're done. Got it?"

The room nodded.

"You're here in case we have to fight our way out."

BRAWLEY WAS LYING on top of his covers, staring out at the moon and stars through the tiny window in their bedroom, when Tucker returned from his shower.

"Sure is a fucked up world, isn't it?" He pulled on his water bottle.

Tucker felt the same way. "That's what we do. We do the stuff no one else can," he answered as he slipped on his boxers. Then he added, "But I agree. It's a mess."

"Makes you wonder if this is going to be our next big Desert Storm thing," said Brawley. His voice reflected disgust.

Tucker didn't agree this time. "Well, let's hope we learned a thing or two. It didn't turn out so well over there for anyone. If I can read what Kyle's told us, we're here to pick out the bad actors and make it so they are removed, arrange it so the rest can work together and get everyone to play nice."

"That would be a miracle. Feels like turf warfare to me. Centuries of it."

"You get enough water down?" Tucker asked.

"I'll be peeing all night long." Brawley held up his near-empty water bottle to show him. "And just in case you wanted to know, I've not missed my meds, either, Dr. Hudson."

"That a boy." He hung up his towel and laid out his

clothes for tomorrow morning. "You mind if I do a little writing before I turn in? I got a book light I can use, but I won't if it bothers you. Or I could use the bathroom."

"Have at it. Won't bother me at all. We get up at seven?"

"That works. Make sure you look for that diaper, Brawley."

But Brawley didn't answer.

Tucker retrieved the notebook Brandy had left him, turned on the small penlight, and opened to a page opposite one of her water color drawings of a bowl of persimmons. He started to write.

Been here for two days now, although it seems like I've been gone a week. This place is very diverse—a splash of cultures, races, and languages. Very colorful, and also very poor. This is a place that has tried to heal over a scar created centuries ago during the dark Slave Coast period. Once powerful countries dominated the culture here, now being swept away and usurped by new tyrants and cultures all trying to impose themselves on this part of the African continent.

It makes me appreciate working plumbing, cell phone service, fast food restaurants, and highways I can drive at ninety miles an hour with the top down just to look at the landscape flying by.

I plan to have a seriously good time with you tonight in this lumpy bed, that is, if Brawley doesn't snore too loud. He's his usual self. I think he's going to be fine.

So while I'm dozing off, I'm going to remember our shower together on Sunday and the way your skin felt under my wet fingers as I rubbed shower gel all over you. I'm going to remember your laugh and the way your hair catches fire in the first light of the morning. I feel lucky to have you and our home to come back to.

Tomorrow we start our adventure, descending into the unknown. It's something that I remember doing before. I won't lie to you and say I'm not a bit fearful. But I'm vigilant. It's that healthy side of being scared—the part that will keep me alive until my time has come.

But, in my wildest dark imagination, I don't see how it's possible I could be given the miracle of loving you just to have it taken it all away. So that's the plan. I'm working my way back to you. And when I get there, I'll be all yours until the next time.

Loving you now more than I ever have, Tucker.

CHAPTER 8

BRANDY DECIDED TO explore her watercolor painting more avidly. She got out several of her old sketch books, looking for shapes and patterns that inspired her. She'd always loved the colorful fruit labels on the boxes at her dad's store and had experimented with drawing some in the bright combinations she'd seen.

She was taking pictures of baskets of red and green apples and vibrant oranges, when she noticed her father speaking with a young woman very privately. It dawned on her that perhaps this was that new element she'd been noticing about her father—his sudden interest in dressing better and his more active lifestyle. He'd been working out at the local gym, something he hadn't done since her mother passed.

At the end of the conversation, he gave the woman a chaste hug and then watched her get into her car and drive away. Before he could look Brandy's way, she turned and busied herself with her photography.

She had followed his actions all afternoon, sorting fruit, arranging bundles of asparagus, and pulling wilted greens, but since he didn't volunteer anything, she didn't ask him about his new friend. She caught him singing under his breath and smiling more to customers, and the other staff. He didn't even mind the constant interruptions by their new bookkeeper's questions and was patient and forthcoming with the answers.

Brandy knew that something or someone had caused this change in him, and she was dying to find out.

"Maybe she's just an old customer," said Dorie. The two of them had taken Jessica to the zoo. The toddler was excitedly watching pink flamingos who had gathered at the side of the path from the safety of her stroller.

"Not the way he was talking to her. And I've never seen him give a hug to a customer before."

"Did it bother you?" Dorie asked.

"No. It was nice." She wished she'd been able to see the woman's face.

"So ask him."

Brandy had to think about this for a few seconds. She and her father lived so close together. They'd both done their best to respect each other's private lives.

She'd never seen him stay out late or have company at the house, but there was something different about the way he acted around this woman.

"I'll wait a bit. Maybe she'll come in soon, and I can do a little reconnaissance first."

"Brandy, you're so funny. Just ask him. Besides, you want to help him out with the vetting. You know there are ladies out there who prey on older men. You don't want him to be taken advantage of. So that's where you're coming from. Just ask him."

Dorie was right. Now that she had married Tucker, the roles had been a bit reversed. She was finding herself more and more the one taking care of her father than the other way around.

The next day, she found him stacking boxes in the back room cooler and asked if she could talk to him.

He closed the heavy metal door, removed his work gloves, and stared back at her with his hands on his hips. "I'm all ears. Something going on with Tucker and the boys?"

She found this amusing, and shrugged. "No, Dad, I wanted to talk about *you*."

"Me? What about me?"

The look he gave her back did have that small twinkle in his eye, like he had already suspected what she was curious about.

"Are you seeing someone?"

She knew she had hit the target when he smiled and looked down at his shoes, rubbing his hands together. His bow tie was crooked. She leaned over and adjusted it before he could step back.

His face flushed with embarrassment. "Thanks, sweetheart." He struggled for words.

"I was going to wait a little longer to say something, but I think this is okay. Yes, I've been seeing someone. Her name is Jillian. I met her at yoga class."

"Yoga? I didn't know you were taking yoga."

"Well, I decided to try it. I mean, I've been watching the class come and go for a few weeks now. You know, I use the equipment on the other side, and I figured they could use a man in there. Lots of ladies. And they didn't seem to mind."

"Didn't seem to mind? I'll bet they were all over you."

He leaned back on his heels, a sheepish grin on his face. "I don't know about that."

"Dad, you're a good-looking man. Or are you just figuring that out?"

Brandy was having fun at his expense.

"So tell me about her."

"She lost her husband only last year. She still wears her wedding ring, as I do. I don't know how the conversation came up, but we discovered we both had lost our spouses."

"Okay. So you like this lady? What does she do?"

"She sells real estate but is kind of part-time. Sort of semi-retired. Her husband left her in good shape, so she dabbles around with lots of things. Has two grown daughters on their own." He looked up. "She's a nice lady. Easy to be around. I guess you could say I'm rather smitten."

Brandy could see he was proud of the admission.

"Does she feel the same way?"

"I think so. Right now, we're just getting to know each other. I'm kind of slow on the romance scale, but neither of us is in a hurry. It's just nice to have someone to talk to, laugh with again. I've missed that, Brandy."

She was delighted with the news and grabbed him in a big bear hug. "I'm so happy for you, Dad. I knew there was something. You've changed, and I like it. I'd say she's a good influence on you."

"Would you like to meet her?"

"Absolutely."

"How about coming over tonight for dinner? I'm barbequing."

"Perfect. I'll bring the wine."

BEFORE BRANDY WENT next door to her father's house to meet this mystery woman, she called Dorie, telling her the news.

"Good old Steve. I'm happy for him. It's about time. He's paid his dues, grieved too long. I'm glad he's found someone. And you like her?"

"I do."

"Well, here's to another happily ever after."

"Indeed. You doing okay, Dorie? I didn't make my calls today, and I'm sorry."

"Well, I just came from the doctor, and I'm pregnant again. Not sure how Brawley will take it this time. God, I wish he was home."

"Me too."

JILLIAN BORDEN WASN'T anything like Brandy's mother, which surprised her. But she was very welcoming and eager to please. She liked to travel, something her father had always liked but her mother had been too ill to do much.

Watching the two of them prepare dinner together in his kitchen, showing her where he kept things and laughing when they bumped into each other, apologizing, Brandy could see they were a good match. She made him happy just by being there. There wasn't any real heavy lifting to do—they just seemed compatible.

It was the kind of relationship she had wanted with Tucker, but then realized she'd married someone completely different than her father. The choices they were going to have to make were much more complicated.

After dinner, she walked to the back of the property, back to her bungalow, took a hot shower, and then turned in early. The silent and empty house made her sad. She hoped very soon she'd be able to hear from him and know that he was well.

She allowed herself one last cry and vowed tomorrow she'd toughen up. But tonight, she missed Tucker more than ever.

CHAPTER 9

J EAN DOUCHET LOOKED *exactly* like a former Special
Forces guy, Tucker thought. He was smaller in
stature, like a lot of the European Spec Ops guys were,
but he had powerful arms and shoulders and he moved
with sleek speed. He could have been mistaken for an
older mixed martial arts guy or even a world-class
triathlete.

Kyle had confided in him Jean had gone through
the BUD/S and SQT training and was one of the
"special relationship" guys who could work out in the
SEAL Team 3 building at Coronado. They'd met
originally when Kyle's platoon was doing training for
the French elite units, and the two had remained
friends.

Jean's eyes picked up every nuance going on in the
room. Tucker met several Eastern European Special
Forces guys who embedded with them for brief missions in the past, and they'd told him knowing multiple

languages fluently meant that they could practically talk to someone in one language and write a text message in another. Not the same message. So Tucker understood that Jean was a giant of an asset for their squad. He admired how detailed he studied all of the American SEALs.

Tucker was certain in less than a few hours Jean would know every team member's personality type better than a therapist would after a year of visits. He was *that* good.

Kyle introduced him without all the background Tucker was privy to, except for something the guys would appreciate.

"Jean has gotten some of our embassy staff out of some pretty prickly situations over the past few years, so you listen to him. He grew up here and then served under the BFST, French Special Forces command in the Middle East and in West Africa, Ivory Coast Command. When he retired, he went private, and we're damned lucky to have him." Kyle stepped away and allowed Douchet to take over.

"*Bonjour, mes amis,*" he started. In his clipped French accent, he explained where they would be traveling and what they should look out for. "When we arrive at the town of Lagos, which is after the border into Nigeria, we'll be heading inland, roughly following the Ogun River. Be sure you have your passports handy to show the border guards or they won't let you through."

Jean heard shouting outside and went to the window to check out what was happening four stories below. "We have demonstrations almost every day here. Mostly small ones, thank goodness." He grinned, and again, the team responded. Tucker could see how he could be charming when he needed to be. He was measured, cultured, and confident.

"I will take the lead vehicle with your chief. The rest of the trucks will be driven by my detail. It will cause less scrutiny that way, since I often accompany NGOs of various countries doing work in the area. My men know the terrain and most of the jungle. I trust them completely. We will all be armed. I'm assuming you are, but don't brandish them or draw attention to them. Just know that people will expect you have them for your personal safety, so don't show off. Be discrete."

Someone asked if his detail spoke English.

"But of course. Probably better than you."

The team chuckled.

"I trained most of them, all dual French and Benin citizenship. They are the best of the best, and they frequently have to turn down offers to work for lots of money in Europe or work as head of security for some of the contractors here. But they love their job, and I don't believe any of them would ever leave working for me. I want you to know who they are before we begin. Don't fuck with my men."

It took a minute for his smile to creep across his chops, but everyone in the room got the message loud and clear.

"Feel free to ask them questions. They will room near your quarters, but downstairs. Everything has been set up for your 'survey and site investigation'," he said, holding his fingers up in the air to show the quotes. "I have done this for others. We will have a secure WIFI connection. I am excited to tell you that this evening, after we arrive, you may be able to do Facetime with some of your families. However, at this time, I need you to stay off your individual cell phones, unless there is some emergency. I'll lay out rules on that."

Kyle had a question. "You expect we'll have to stop along the way? Or be stopped? And if so, what will we need to say?"

"That's an excellent question, Kyle. Only at the border. If we're lucky!" When no one laughed, he added, "That was a joke!"

Tucker felt his blood pressure rise.

"In otherwords, if you get stopped before the border, something has gone wrong."

"Gotcha. Thanks, Jean." Kyle retreated to the side

and then took up a chair.

"I know I don't have to mention to you that you should not speak unless you are asked a question, and then you are very polite or say very respectfully you don't understand. Let my boys do the talking. *All* the talking."

After they were released, Tucker followed as he was directed, riding in the second seat next to Brawley behind their huge African driver, Leone. Trace and Tyler sat behind them, crammed into the third seat. Their truck towed a small trailer which contained the inflatable combat Zodiac and the small 55 cc super lightweight diesel motor that he'd been told had been customized for speed. The whole thing could fit into a man's backpack if need be.

Tyler retrieved waters from the back and passed them along up front. The convoy began to roll out and blended into traffic.

Tucker addressed Leone's eyes, visible in the rear-view mirror. "How long will it take to get there?"

Leone shrugged, fanning the fingers of his right hand to show him it was an approximation. "We go about four to five hours. Depends on traffic, road work."

Tucker noted the man's perfect English. He nodded and thanked him.

Leone continued. "We always got road work. Lots

of rain. Landslides. Big trucks. It's a constant problem. This time of year, not too bad."

Everyone was silent on the trip down the coast, where Tucker saw breathtaking stretches of white rocky beach snuggling up against blue waters like the Caribbean. Yet around the next bend could be dark brown granite cliffs without a hospitable landing area. At the water's edge of one azure blue bay, a hole had been dug and overflowed with reddish brown mud, which spilled out into the pristine bay, marring it with a brown stain feathering out to the ocean.

Occasionally, there would be iron security gates leading down to a luxuriously landscaped, western-style hotel or villa, but then next to it, they would come upon a crumbling structure or something that had burned and been repaired with metal corrugated siding and cinder block. Children walked dangerously close to the road on their way to school, dressed in their uniforms.

Clusters of tiny shops, gas stations, and wooden fruit stands roofed with palm fronds dotted the inland side of the coast, often accompanied by a couple of bars or liquor stores. Less than half of these were open. Groups of men sat together in the shade smoking, squatting on the dusty ground or sitting on oil drums or plastic buckets. The locals shared the ground with chickens who dodged traffic, bicycles, and scooters, while foraging for food. Fabrics in bright, bold designs and dresses blew in the breeze at wooden makeshift shops manned by women in colorful dress, often talking with one or two other ladies or children.

Their audiences, one by one, passively watched the caravan pass by and then refocused on whatever they were doing. Several scooters overloaded with as many as three children zipped dangerously around the traffic, pitching precariously and nearly spilling their precious cargo. Men and women balanced huge bundles atop their heads.

Tucker soaked all the visuals up, allowed the drone of the motor and bouncing of the Land Rover's squeaky shocks to lull him to near sleep. At one point, he did fall asleep and spilled water in his lap.

The patchwork of colors and textures was so unfamiliar yet strangely beautiful, even though the heat was oppressive. He could smell fires burning and felt the grit in his teeth from sitting by the opened window inhaling road dust. He was looking forward to a shower already and they had traveled no more than two hours.

At several points along the way they'd encounter a tall pile of debris—lumber, poles, broken bricks and chunks of concrete and plaster—with children and young men going through the rubble, mining for something they could sell. Advertisements for beer, sodas, political candidates long gone, and even cell phone and internet services were plastered to walls, fences, and sometimes, palm trees.

A billboard announced they were approaching the border with Nigeria. The picture contained the image of a black fist rising to the heavens with a green and yellow flag waving in the background. The convoy slowed and then stopped at the archway crossing. Everywhere Tucker looked he saw uniformed men in light blue shirts and navy or black pants, most of them with sub machine guns at their sides or long rifles strapped to their backs.

Tucker took his passport out of his vest pocket.

The two border guards at Kyle and Jean's vehicle slowly slid their sunglasses to their foreheads and peered inside their truck. Soon, two more did the same at Tucker's vehicle. Leone spoke an African dialect to the guard on his left, who then wanted to check out Tucker's passport and then handed it back. The guard on Brawley's side craned his neck and did the same, asking for Tyler and Trace's passports as well. Then both guards walked the length of the truck, studying what they could see inside the cab. Tucker was pleased to note someone had remembered to bring the two fishing poles they'd purchased, along with the net, which lay on top of their suitcases.

Jean and Kyle went inside the small border guard

office secured with a glass door that had been taped back together with duct tape. Traffic coming into Benin was completely blocked off with barricades until the guards were done checking out all the Areva Afrique trucks and their occupants. Several other guards stood idly by and watched without saying a word.

The heat was oppressive with the complete lack of wind present. Leone tried to find a tune on the radio and finally gave up. He tapped his fingers on the roof of the truck, humming some Juju beat tune they'd heard in the city yesterday. A large tourist bus, which had been held up in the now-growing line of cars waiting to enter Benin, honked his horn.

"Oh, mister," whispered Leone. "Not a good idea, mister." Leone leaned over the seat, turned, and said to Tucker, "Chinese."

"Chinese tourists?" Tucker asked.

"No. Workers. They take them from the airport to their apartments. Then they take them to work, and back to the apartments. They do not wander in the villages."

"Are they held captive?" Brawley asked.

"You would say so, yes. But they are very quiet and very hard workers. If they cannot leave their compounds, they don't have a problem, right?"

"Where are they working?" Tucker asked.

"Mostly construction. They work on roads, even built a small private air strip."

"A friendship project, right?" said Tucker.

"Exactly."

They were given the green light to move forward, and their caravan continued down the coast until they encountered a fairly large city. Tucker read the signs and figured they would be heading away from the coastal areas, going inland. The road wove through various neighborhoods until it came to an expansive city center, designed with wide streets and fountains.

"Dada's folly," Leone said.

"Looks like Barcelona," Patrick said.

"This is Lagos. One of our early presidents, Dada, envisioned building a modern-day Babylon during the sixties. He nearly bankrupted the country with this project. But in the day, it was remarkable."

Once out of the city, they turned off the provincial highway and traveled a compacted red dirt road, which was slow and filled with potholes. Leone maneuvered as best he could, being mindful of the trailer they were pulling. Dust from Kyle's truck nearly obscured them. Lush jungle foliage appeared to have been burned back from the road to allow passage. They were coming to a small rise.

Once they hit the plateau, the view down to the coast was breathtaking. The air was slightly cooler but thick with mosquitos, especially as they approached the Ogun River. Dark-legged Sandpiper-looking birds with black and white racoon-like mask markings walked along the water's edge, wading several inches deep for food. Tucker observed a flock of bright red canaries and a bright blue bird the size and shape of a robin.

But the most amazing thing Tucker found was that he could hear the cacophony of bird calls, even above their groaning diesel engine.

They crossed the Ogun several times and, at last, came to a series of small towns to the south of Abeokuta, the region's capitol. The district was heavy with two- and three-story industrial buildings, mostly made of concrete and cinder block.

After several minutes traveling the narrow road through remote jungle, they turned off onto a crushed stone drive ending at a security gate without any signage whatsoever. The perimeter was fenced with heavy-gauge electrical fencing reaching over twenty feet tall. The gate automatically opened and closed behind them as they continued crossing what appeared to be a large private compound. A massive stone building loomed three stories tall, set in the middle of a grassy knoll, its rooftop covered in satellite dishes and several multistory antennae. They parked as directed by a security guard who greeted them.

Tucker could hardly get out of the Rover, he was so stiff. Every bounce, curve, and swerve had taken a toll on his body. Brawley laughed as Jameson and Patrick could hardly extricate themselves from the third seat as well.

All the Areva Afrique vehicles were lined up side by side, and the team was ushered around the front and up several steps, stopping at a massive porch overhang with a view of the knoll below and the Ogun River beyond the fencing farther down. Each member carried his own bag, and one by one, they dropped them to stare out at the beauty of the majestic scene.

"Holy shit," mumbled Fredo. "We the private guests of a king or something?"

Kyle shrugged.

"Nice, isn't it?" Jean remarked.

Surveying the lush green on the other side of the river, Tucker didn't see evidence of another structure. They appeared to be completely isolated.

Enormous carved wooden doors opened to the interior of the building. Inside was a nearly empty, two-story lobby containing a curved wooden reception desk that appeared to be hand crafted from a single tree trunk, skillfully carved in relief depicting leaves, vines and various symmetric symbols and shapes.

The almost black, highly polished granite floors echoed eerily. Several members whistled while others whispered astonishment. Tucker felt like he'd just walked into a brand-new museum.

Jean walked to the middle of the crowd and began his orientation. "This is probably the safest place in all of Nigeria, impervious to most rocket attacks and even perhaps some air strikes. The walls are made of reinforced concrete nearly two feet thick. As you probably saw, we have a satellite uplink and a dedicated, secure WIFI system, so you'll be able to call home as soon as we finish the activation tonight. In the meantime, there are offices upstairs that have been set up with beds. There's a large lounge area where we've got several big screen TVs so you aren't cut off from the world. We hope all the other things will be working by tomorrow."

"What was this built for?" asked Tucker.

"Originally, it was built with money from the Soviets about twenty years ago, designed to house the government safely in case of a military coup. Sort of a safe house. They chose the location because it's well away from the country's capitol but connected by a waterway to the coast. Even got room for a few helicopters in an emergency. You could easily stage an invasion from this place, and perhaps that's what they had in mind. It's nearly two hundred thousand square feet. We were able to purchase it several years ago to be used by our government and corporate clients."

Jean's men began unloading boxes of supplies, including all the duty bags containing their weapons.

"We have a large kitchen downstairs in the back, and we have one of my guys coming to prepare meals, so keep your equipment out of sight in your rooms."

"This is huge. Very unexpected," said Kyle.

"It's way more than you need, of course, but I'm afraid it's the safest place I can put you right now. You're close enough to the city, where a lot of your research will be done, and only a few paces to the river. Most people in this area don't even know this building exists, and those that do, understand it's a space rented out for corporate events. You probably won't be bothered here since this road is not on any map, by design."

"Are you staying here with us?" someone asked.

"I'm going to stay with my men. We're taking the downstairs right wing. You guys have the top floor. Go check it out, and then I need to get upriver with your boat crew before it gets dark."

The men explored the upper floor and set up their rooms, sticking to the original roommate list. Only thing Tucker could complain about was that there weren't private baths. But Brawley found the real prize.

"You guys won't believe this!" he shouted. He opened two six-foot glass doors behind him, revealing a multi-station working gym with newer equipment. Beyond was a full locker room complete with a row of stall showers, toilets, and even a steam room.

"I think someone slipped me some LSD," said T.J.

Tucker completely agreed. It was the most unlikely outcome to their hot and dusty road trip down the coast.

CHAPTER 10

B RANDY'S CELL PHONE rang as she was just about to
put on her green apron.

"Hey there, beautiful!"

She couldn't believe her ears.

"Turn on your camera so I can see you."

She stared down into the phone screen and saw
Tucker's smiling face looking right back at her. "Oh my
god! I can't believe it's you!"

"Of course, it's me."

"What time is it there?"

"About five. I think we're eight hours ahead."

"So how's it going?"

"You wouldn't believe me if I told you. Trust me on
this."

"Really?" He looked good, not at all stressed. She
expected to see a sweaty and dirty version of him, like
how he was when he worked in the garden or fixed
things around the house, but Tucker was clean and

appeared to be calling from a swanky office.

"You sure you're in Africa? I think you guys just took off for Vegas. That's what it looks like to me."

Brawley walked behind Tucker and waved.

"Hey, Brawley!"

"He's next. We got a line here. Anyway, I can't take too much time because a lot of us are lined up to check in at home, so this is just a quick one. Wanted you to know I'm alive, we are all situated, and so far, everything's been better than I expected. The real work begins tomorrow, though, so fingers crossed."

"Oh, thank you for calling, Tucker. I've been missing you so much, trying not to be worried, but I took your advice and have been staying busy."

"Good job. Well, I have to—"

"Wait a minute. I have news! I mean Dad does. He's met someone, Tucker. I had dinner with them last night. They are so cute together. I think you'll like her."

"Happy to hear it, sweetheart. But I've gotta go."

She threw him a kiss, which he returned. Just before he hung up, he told her he'd call longer tomorrow, if he could. "And I'm dreaming of you naked," he whispered. It generated some catcalls around him.

Brandy slipped her shirt over one shoulder to show him the only part of her bare skin she could. "You get your butt back here, Tucker. I mean it."

"Roger that, ma'am."

With that, he disconnected. She placed the phone in her center apron pocket and felt like she'd just had about a dozen cups of coffee. Then she wished she'd recorded the call and decided she'd ask one of the younger clerks how to do that for next time.

She was happy Brawley was going to get in touch with Dorie. She needed some cheering up. Brandy decided to check in with her in an hour, so she didn't interfere with Brawley's call. She wondered if her friend was going to tell her husband about the upcoming pregnancy.

Her father came around the corner with a cart filled with cardboard boxes of plump yellow peaches that looked delicious.

"I just got a call from Tucker, Dad. He's fine, got there safe. And he looks great!" She hugged him so fast she nearly toppled the peaches.

"That's great news, Brandy. Must mean a load off your mind. Did he say anything about where he was or what he was doing?"

"He can't say. Even Brawley looked good."

"Makes me happy to see that big smile on your face. I'll tell Jillian tonight. She'll be thrilled."

AFTER BRANDY FINISHED going through the mail, she handed the stack of bills back to their bookkeeper for entry. She was going to call Dorie, but her best friend beat her to it.

"Brawley just called me. You got to talk to Tucker?"

"Yes! They look good, don't they?"

"Oh man, it was just what I needed."

"Did he get to talk to Jessica too?"

"No, she was sleeping. He told me it was going to be short this time. But we're going to try to get a schedule so she can be up for his calls. He said they're staying in this super-secret compound. Did Tucker say anything like that?"

"No. He wouldn't talk about it."

"Well, we've got to celebrate. How about I get a sitter and we go to the movies?"

"I'm up for that. Text me what time. I can pick you up."

Brandy met Dorie at Danny and Luci's house, where she'd dropped off Jessica. It was the first time she'd met Danny's wife. Her long shiny black hair was parted down the middle, framing her beautiful face with kind, dark eyes.

Brandy was introduced to Griffin and Ali, their two boys. Luci explained that Griffin was Danny and Luci's biological son, but Ali was an adopted Iraqi boy Danny had rescued on one of their missions. The team had tried to rescue both he and his father, but his father sacrificed himself to save the boy.

"The boys have been looking forward to it." Luci

said. "I need to give them girl time, teach them some manners about being gentle with little girls. We don't get much chance to do that around here."

"Tell her about the sling shot," said Dorie.

Luci inhaled, first checking to make sure everyone was playing nice behind her. "Well, Danny made this sling shot for Ali over in Iraq and taught him how to shoot pebbles. Turns out, he's a crack shot! But the problem is, poor Griffin, who's not so adventurous, has had more goose eggs and black eyes than any other four-year-old around. Ali likes to lay in wait and pummel him. We've bought him some sponge balls to use, but he likes the real thing. Shoots jam and sugar packets at the waitresses, too, when we go out. Drives me insane!"

Brandy couldn't stop laughing.

They heard a loud, "No!" coming from behind Luci. No mistaking Jessica's voice.

"Oh boy. I better check—" started Dorie.

"No, they're fine." Luci held her hand out. "Whatever it is, we'll sort it out no problem. You have a good time and I'll call or text you if something comes up I can't handle, okay?"

"Thanks." Dorie gave Luci a hug.

"How's Danny?" Brandy asked.

"Thank God for that call. I was beginning to worry, but man, some of the places they go are mind boggling.

Sounds like this trip won't be any different. It was great to see his face."

"Yeah, I guess next one we'll get more details," said Brandy.

"You may not know this, but Danny's cousin Wilson, is on his first deployment with them. He's a SWCC boat guy."

"Yes, Dorie told me."

"Thanks again, Luci," repeated Dorie. "We'll let you know when we're on our way home. I'm leaving my car here with the car seat. Do you want the keys?"

"No, I have two in mine. Have a great time."

AFTER THE MOVIE let out, Dorie checked on Jessica and was told they were all crashed, so the two of them stopped by one of the places on the strand for some soup.

Groups of young men, mostly Navy and not all of them SEALs, hung out around the outdoor fireplace, watching the girls sauntering by. It was a parade that had been going on for decades, ever since the SEALs had come to such public prominence. Brandy could see it was quite the show this evening. Young, skimpily-clad girls roamed between several of the local hangouts and especially flocked around the quiet tatted guys with the big arms. Brandy guessed by the difference in their demeanor they were probably SEALs.

Couples sat together at smaller tables around the perimeter. The air hadn't turned chilly yet, and the sky was clear. A large bachelorette party had taken up the long picnic table at the far side and were boisterous, at times drowning out conversations on the whole patio. The bride-to-be wore a short white veil with plastic penises attached, a crown, and a sash. Falling victim to drinks purchased for her by several of the guy groups, she was thoroughly smashed and had to be helped out when the party decided to move. Brandy sensed the entire place was relieved.

"Remember when we'd come down here in high school?" queried Dorie.

"Well, you came down. I was your comic relief." Brandy thought about how long ago it was. "And for the record, you weren't a sloppy drunk at your bachelorette party, either."

"Thank you," Dorie said, and clinked her water glass with Brandy's beer.

"You ever see the girls? The bridesmaids?"

"Not really. Funny how you know who your true friends are." She grasped Brandy's hand. "You've always been the one there for me, Brandy. I appreciate it."

Brandy remembered the wedding and how the other girls in the wedding party had treated her, made her feel excluded. How they stared when Tucker spilled the punch all over her. She'd been so embarrassed she almost left the reception. But she stayed, and it changed her whole life. She couldn't help but break out in a wicked grin.

"What the devil are you thinking, Brandy Hudson?"

She loved to gloat, especially when it felt like justice done. "They all went to the wedding to pick up one of Brawley's friends, didn't they?"

"Oh, it was the only thing they talked about!"

"Even your married bridesmaid—her guy is on Team 5?"

"Oh, Marsha. Yes, she's a slut."

Brandy pushed aside her soup bowl and leaned onto the table. "But I'm the one who went home with one. I'm the one who got the SEAL!"

"Poetic justice. As it should be. You got the best one of the bunch, too, except for Brawley, of course." Dorie winked.

Brandy was glad some of the darkness of their relationship seemed to be fading. She wished for more of that magic for Dorie and Brawley she'd envied when they first fell in love and became engaged.

A group of slightly older ladies sat at the table nearby without paying attention to anything in the room but the men scattered across the patio. Dorie studied them with a frown. Brandy could tell the ladies were trying to hook attention from one particular group of well-built guys she guessed were SEALs.

Dorie leaned forward. "You want to go?"

Brandy agreed and slipped her purse over her shoulder. One of the ladies at the next table called out to Dorie, who didn't look especially happy to see her. The woman scampered over and gave her a hug.

"You old married lady, you. Congratulations! Why didn't you invite me to the wedding? And how the heck is Brawley?"

The dark-haired woman was beautiful and very well-endowed, but she used a little too much eye makeup, Brandy thought. Her comparison engine had kicked in, and she sucked in her tummy, allowing anyone who wasn't blind to see that her chest was bigger than this woman's. Brandy also noticed that her eyes were hard.

"He's fine," answered Dorie, turning to go. Brandy thought it was odd she didn't offer an introduction but dutifully followed after her friend, turning to go, when they heard the woman ask a question.

"And how's Tucker?" Her sexy voice was laced with a growl.

Dorie closed her eyes, bit her lower lip, and then mouthed "sorry" to Brandy before she turned and addressed the woman. "Tucker married Brandy about two years ago, Shayla."

Shayla's head whipped to the side as she thoroughly studied Brandy up and down. After gaining her composure, the woman tilted her head back and whispered her reply. "Oh my." She leaned closer to Brandy with a smirk. "Tucker and I were married seven years," she said as she extended her hand. "I'm Shayla." The smile followed her greeting instead of preceding it.

"Nice to meet you." Brandy's handshake was short. In the next few awkward seconds, she had the urge to wipe her hand on her dress. Out of nowhere, she threw in a comment she knew she'd burn in hell for. Tucker would be furious with her, but she just couldn't hold her tongue—why she'd been fired from her last two jobs. Adjusting her stance, she said, "Thanks for divorcing him."

Before Shayla could respond verbally, Dorie interjected that they were late to pick up her daughter. She grabbed Brandy's arm and dragged her back into the protection of the bar.

As she disappeared, Brandy gave a taunting wave at the woman she knew instantly she hated. She suspected it would come back to haunt her.

But it was worth it.

CHAPTER 11

W HILE THE REST of the team was having dinner, Tucker was selected to take the river trip with Jean, Kyle, and the two boat crew guys.

The Zodiac was inflated while Wilson lovingly wiped down the compact motor he'd boosted, carefully attaching it to the craft. Everyone helped position the craft into the water, carrying it over the debris-laden and rocky bank. One tug on the starting rope and the engine kicked over and purred, sounding more like a small chainsaw than an outboard motor.

Everyone boarded, stashing their duty bags at their feet. They were instructed to pack light, which meant no heavy firepower and nothing a local businessman or government contractor wouldn't normally carry for a trip of this nature. Jean handed Kyle a sat phone for security since it would be impossible to trace and would give him direct access to the SOF command as well as Jean and his team, at all times.

They pushed off, heading upriver. Tucker felt just like when he and his dad went hunting in Oregon when he was a boy. The water was filled with debris, including plastic wrappers, floating foam cups, and occasionally an article of clothing. Depending on how close to the center of the waterway they were, the color of the river went from shit brown to brownish green. He was glad he wore his goggles around his neck, since, if he had to swim in the water, his eyes would most likely get infected.

Even though he'd applied repellant, the mosquitos had found him. He fought off the first few but then ignored them in time, like Jean did.

The French former Spec Ops guy searched the banks with his binoculars. Birds were at full play, chattering up a storm. They motored past a squabbling family of medium-sized brown and yellow monkeys moving along the treetops with ease. Several of the males began to follow along the trajectory of the boat and then broke off.

Carson was point, holding a long pole and sounding the river floor, on the lookout for large boulders or any other impediment to travel. Wilson manned the motor, steering to keep them in the center of the river and away from water plants that hugged the sides and could interfere with the small motor.

"I'm assuming we are to watch for crocs?" asked

Kyle.

"To be sure," said Jean. "Not too many in these areas as many of them are harvested for their meat and sold at market."

"Appreciate the head's up, Chief," Carson shouted over his shoulder.

They continued upstream for several more minutes and then followed a sharp bend to the right.

Jean sat straight up with a command. "Carson, sometimes the Ogun dries up overnight, so be especially vigilant for shallow straits." he barked.

Carson gave him a thumbs-up in answer, not taking his eyes off the water.

Tucker took another admiring appraisal of the tiny diesel engine and smiled up at Wilson. "That thing sure does sound pretty," he said. "That a fifty-five?"

"Yup, but we got twenty percent more torque. Best little twenty-five-pound bundle out there. I can stick it in my backpack and carry the darned thing all day if I had to."

"I'm impressed. You do all the work?"

"I don't let anyone else touch this baby. Can't wait to demonstrate how she'll do full out. Covers the bank with waves about eight feet or more."

"Cool beans."

Jean was checking his phone and then spoke to someone on the other end in French. He put his binoculars up and checked the bank ahead while he continued the conversation, finishing it off with, *"Oui. Bon."*

Kyle was waiting for an explanation.

"We have a camp around the bend here that appears abandoned, but we're supposed to check it out on foot. Then I think we'll head back. I was going to try for the city, but I don't want to take a chance and get caught after dark."

"What kind of camp?" asked Kyle.

"My guy thinks they're smugglers."

Several minutes later, a clearing was visible where the jungle foliage had been hacked down and piled up. Evidence of off-road trails led into the thick foliage at the perimeter. Jean pointed to a fallen tree that was jutting out into the river, and Wilson positioned the boat to come in close, reducing the engine to a near stop. Jean searched the bank for evidence of inhabitants and then finally gave Wilson the okay to shut down the motor.

Carson guided the boat, acting as the bumper to avoid brushing up against anything sharp. He braced for the landing, secured the craft to the fallen stump, and then was the first to jump out into the shallow water where he attached another line.

Everyone hopped out, fanning into position around the clearing. Tucker first explored the tall grasses at the perimeter, looking through debris scattered in the brush as Jean and Kyle slipped in and out of the jungle, exploring the recently-made trails.

Carson called Kyle over to the riverbank.

"What you got?"

"Just showing you there's been another boat here recently, sir. It's a solid hull, probably a metal jitney. See how it left grooves in the mud?"

"Thanks for pointing that out, Carson. Good observation." Kyle returned to the camp perimeter.

Tucker found a plastic lidded box that had been tossed aside and then covered with branches. He put on his gloves and carefully set the container down at his feet. Inside were miscellaneous pill bottles, some vials of antibiotic, gauze, and some sports wrap tape. An opened box of latex gloves had spilled at the bottom. Kyle was at his side in an instant.

"I could use some of these things, leave them at the compound," Tucker advised.

"Are they still good? What are they?" Kyle wondered.

Tucker rummaged through the bottles carefully. "We got penicillin tablets, something for malaria, some aspirin, and these vials of antibiotic. Nothing to inject with and no pain killers, though."

Jean had joined the little circle.

"What do you think, Tucker?" asked Kyle.

"Looks like a medic kit, but without the pain killers and the needles. My guess is someone kept them and discarded everything else."

"Does the lid have a label?" asked Jean.

Tucker held it up, showing a label had been removed.

"You have a problem if he keeps this?" Kyle asked Jean.

Jean shrugged. "If you can use it, no."

Tucker set the box near the shore and moved on to the firepit, kneeling to see if he could recognize anything that had been burned there. He could still feel heat coming up, but there were no embers or fire. Jean dug around in the ash with a long stick. He hooked a wafer-thin piece of fabric a few inches long, holding it in front of Tucker's face.

"Someone's been burning bandages," he told Jean. "See the borders here? Those are blood stains."

Jean nodded solemnly. "See if you can find more. I'm going to alert the others."

Tucker removed the surface debris with his Ka-Bar then dug into the soft ash. He immediately encountered an article he thought at first was a piece of buried food, stabbing it with his knife. But when he laid it on a smooth rock and poured water over it, he discovered that what he'd uncovered was a charred human hand. It was small but not small enough to be that of a child.

It appeared to belong to a woman and was severed cleanly. He noticed the smooth surface of the two cleaved bones above the wrist and associated circular saw marks, which confirmed his suspicions.

"Over here!" Tucker shouted.

Kyle and the others ran to join him.

"This was removed by a surgeon's tool, a portable circular saw," he told Kyle.

Jean knelt down to examine the hand. "Doesn't appear to be an amputation for an infected wound, am I correct?" he asked Tucker.

Tucker nodded. With his gloves still on, he examined the fingers, carefully. He noted a slight indentation, indicating the owner might have worn a ring on the fourth finger. "You see it?" he asked Jean.

The former commando agreed.

Tucker tried to straighten the curled fingers. The nails were charred completely off, leaving black flaky residue, but Tucker discovered that a portion of the little finger had been removed between the second and third joints. This was not done with precision but by hacking the end of the finger off with a small hatchet or knife, perhaps a pair of wire cutters. He looked up at Kyle.

"Proof of life," his chief murmured.

"Or, a trophy perhaps?" added Jean.

Tucker applied more water until he sloughed off

the burned flesh and found enough remaining to make a stunning pronouncement.

"This woman, or young girl, was white."

The hand was wrapped in gauze and bagged after Tucker took pictures. The day's light was rapidly disappearing, and Jean requested they hustle their way home. Tucker tossed the bagged evidence in the plastic kit and carried it to the raft. Jean tapped his shoulder before they fired up the engine.

"Don't leave it in there. Put that in your duty bag and keep it zipped, just in case we get stopped."

"Roger that."

The images of the camp and the torture or possible loss of life haunted him during the return. He suspected it affected the boat guys as well. No one said a word, but they all kept a vigilant eye out for anyone in the brush. When the familiar shore and their building came into view, Tucker breathed a sigh of relief. Together, they carried the raft inside the gated compound, where it was covered in a large green tarp and strapped down.

"Tucker," Jean said after they unpacked their gear. "Go get some dinner, if you're hungry, but put your sample in the freezer for now."

"Will do."

"Oh and, Tucker, be sure to label it."

Tucker gave the former commando a grin. "I think

I'll double bag it, too."

Jenn shrugged. "Would sure be a shame if your mates took that thing out and barbequed it, now wouldn't it?"

Tucker laughed on the outside, but privately recalled stories of some of their Desert Storm Ranger brethren who had gone over the bend in Iraq and created a whole ceremony surrounding roasting ears of the enemy. As a newbie SEAL, he'd had nightmares about it for weeks afterwards.

LATER THAT EVENING, Tucker was catching up in his journal when Brawley came to bed.

"Was wondering where you went," he said.

"Ollie and I watched a couple movies in the stash Wilson brought. Someone went to the trouble to bring us some world-class porn."

A red flag launched in Tucker's brain. Maybe it was his imagination, but he smelled alcohol.

"I hope Kyle didn't catch you drinking."

"Just a couple of shots of Jack. No biggie." Brawley didn't make eye contact.

Tucker decided to let it slide since the hour was still early for a normal working day. But he still didn't like it.

Brawley grabbed his towel and headed to the showers.

Tucker refocused on his notebook which had become a welcomed nighttime routine. He found it easier to write than to talk about his feelings. He figured it was safe, because if he got disgusted with himself for getting gushy, he could just burn the damn book. But without any way of knowing how to post a letter to her, or even knowing if it was allowed, it was all he had available.

He also wanted to purge his brain of the images of the severed hand they'd found today.

Today's trip made me feel grateful we live where we do. I see the violence, the way some people live, and the poverty. It's the same all over the world. One thing for adults to have to fend for themselves, but seeing the little kids having to live in these conditions really gets to me.

I used to think it would be a good idea to think of home and all the wonderful things I'd get back to, but I've changed my mind. I think about those barefoot kids, running around dirty streets, tugging at their mother's skirts, and playing with dusty plastic pans and sticks instead of toys. I think of the killings going on and the danger lurking in the jungle and wonder: when do those kids get to be kids? And it's not war that's doing it. It's desperate poverty and a power struggle that has been going on for centuries.

Seems like a crying shame.

We're staying in a large bunker, sort of a safe house. I can't tell you any more about it, but you'd be pleased to know I'm safe at night, rather than hanging out in a tent in the bush. We even got hot showers and flush toilets!

But you don't care about all that. You just want to know how I'm doing, and let me tell you, I miss you more tonight than ever before.

Now, if I was king of the world, I'd command everyone to fall in love, like I have. I'd make sure they grabbed someone for a hug, not out of fear, but because they wanted to express that love. That would be a perfect world. And it has nothing to do with politics or power.

I guess I have to settle for the fact that what I'm doing is helping some place become more stable so those tiny flames of opportunity and freedom can get kindled, fostered, and become a bonfire. I don't want to run it, and God knows we shouldn't either.

Okay, enough philosophy. I know you can feel my words, Brandy. There's no doubt in my mind about that. You're here with me.

Always.

He put away his light and the notebook, tucking it under his pillow, and slipped down under the covers just before Brawley returned. He tried to push the visions of today from his head, bringing Brandy's smiling face into view, but he fell asleep before her lips could touch his.

CHAPTER 12

THERE WASN'T ANY amount of talking that could settle Brandy's nerves. Dorie explained several times how she should just focus on how much Tucker loved her. Her friend insisted he was a changed man, that she'd never seen him so full of life and happy. Dorie recounted what little she knew of Shayla, especially how manipulating that woman could be. She said not to worry.

Of course, she knew Dorie was telling her the truth. But Brandy still couldn't put it away. She was still fighting back for all the injustices that had been done to her in the past.

"Seriously, Brandy. You have nothing to worry about with Tucker. And, the more you let it get to you, the more she'll get permanently lodged deep in your head. She's not a nice person. That's why I didn't even want you two to be introduced."

"Logically, I know you're right, Dorie. But this obsession with her has got me caught in a rut. You know how it is when you can't get some damned song out of your head?"

"Maybe look at your past as your training, giving you courage to love a man like Tucker. As you've seen, this isn't an easy life, being married to a SEAL. Not everyone can do it. But it's worth it."

Yes, she'd told herself these very things over and over again. Still, she couldn't get the look of this woman out of her thoughts. The knowledge that someone had been private and intimate with her husband—yes, before he was her husband—was driving her crazy. She was so worried she would lose this wonderful relationship or that she could actually damage it just with her fears.

Brandy found no comfort in stacking shelves and clerking at her father's store since he was talking non-stop about all the plans he was making with Jillian. They were going to take a cruise. She was a wonderful cook. She loved to get dirty in the garden with him. All these things were now annoying to her, and it wasn't fair to him to be hanging around.

She asked for, and got, a few days off, so she took a watercolor class at the local community college. But drawing bowls of fruit and fruit labels only made her think about her father's store, which in turn made her think about her father's new romance. It did take her mind off not receiving another call from Tucker.

She knew it was wrong not to be happy for her dad's new relationship.

Dorie told her that Cooper's wife, Libby, had nearly completed her counseling degree, and her dad was the unofficial team head shrink, which Brandy knew. Dorie suggested Brandy call her.

Libby called her right back. "Let's get some lunch. I drop the kids off at school in the morning. Will doesn't get out until three, and Gillian's out at two."

"Perfect. Where?"

They agreed to meet at her favorite seafood place overlooking the harbor, where Tucker had taken her that last afternoon before he left for Africa.

Libby glanced around the wood-paneled bistro, decorated with surfboards, aloha shirts, and posters. "God, I haven't been here in years. We used to come here all the time. Coop had a motorhome he parked down at the beach a way south. The guys affectionally called it the *Babemobile*."

Brandy hadn't heard that story and asked her to explain.

"Cooper is very frugal. He stayed there for pennies, pocketing the Navy's housing allowance. And he could watch the sunsets, run or swim in the surf, and, well, meet girls."

Libby's blushing cheeks lit up her whole face.

Libby continued, "They change. I mean, they're the same person, but more settled with themselves. The first time I saw Coop I didn't want to have anything to do with him."

"Really? Now see, my reaction with Tucker was exactly the opposite, but then, you're like Dorie. Probably never had to worry about a date or about a guy not calling you back."

Libby took a sip of her iced tea and slowly looked up. "Brandy, that's not something you should keep telling yourself. I totally understand that you do…However, contrary to what you might think, I've had some problems with learning to trust men myself. I experienced sexual assault in college with a professor."

"What did you do?"

Libby returned an evil grin. "I got him fired."

"Good for you." She wanted to choose her words carefully. "I know Tucker's not interested in anyone else, and I also know he's glad they split up—"

"But? I know there's a but in there somewhere," Libby pried.

"I think his ex-wife still likes him."

Libby cocked her head. "I'd only worry if he's flattered by that. Does he give any indication it makes him feel good knowing she cares for him? Because a man like that can't be trusted. I don't get that about Tucker, and I barely remember his former wife."

"No, I think he wants to stay as far enough away as possible. I believe him about that."

"So it's not him that you don't trust. It's her? Is that what you're saying?"

"Exactly." As she thought about it further, she corrected herself. "No, it's *me* I don't trust, I guess. I worry I'll make a complete fool of myself on one of those long-distance conference calls. He deserves better, especially now."

"I think you're onto something there." Libby leaned forward and put her hand on Brandy's right hand. "But don't feel like you have to sugar-coat those calls. We're not all happy, happy, happy all the time, are we? Just be honest yet respectful of the pressures he's under."

"So I should focus on trusting myself instead?"

"Here's what I'd tell you to do, and take this with a grain of salt, because I didn't sit for my test nor do I see patients. Think about all the things about you Tucker loves. Remember those things. You are unique. He loves that about you. You speak your mind. He absolutely loves that about you, I can tell! He doesn't want a doormat or someone he has to battle with all the time. He's battling bad guys every day at his job. And he doesn't care about what other women from his past think of him. He just cares about how *you* love him. That's what you show him."

Brandy could tell she'd received very well-timed advice.

Libby continued. "There's a story I hear the guys talk about all the time. They say there are these two dogs. One is a mean dog and the other is a loyal and good dog. You feed the good dog, so he's big and healthy. Don't feed your fears, Brandy. Feed what's good in your life."

BRANDY WAS OVERWHELMED with Libby's gift. She could hardly wait to talk to Tucker the next time and prayed it was soon.

CHAPTER 13

KYLE AND JEAN gave a team update at breakfast. Jean's men had joined them.

"Honest to God, gents, I've been asked three times already this morning about *The Hand*. Well, here it is." He held up the bundle Tucker had wrapped in a tea towel. Tucker hoped it was still frozen.

"You guys are sometimes are like a bunch of teen girls with your gossip. If you weren't told about this, then don't read anything into it. We're doing a lot of stuff here. Nobody is being left out, okay?"

Several of the men nodded. Tucker wondered who had talked about their excursion last night, because he didn't say a word. By the way Wilson had hung his head, he guessed where the leak came from. Not that it was a leak.

Kyle continued, "But just to set the record straight, we found this hand when we went upriver to go check on some intelligence about a group of possible smugglers set up nearby. We confirmed that they had indeed been there and recently."

Jean barged in. "Kyle was tasked with this larger group for a reason. Our efforts might go in several directions. As he has explained to you, it might even take more than one trip for your guys. We figured the more guys we expose to the mission, the better chance we have of long-term success. With that comes some inherent problems. Information that is 'guessed' about can be damaging and downright inaccurate. We want to be able to make split-second decisions based on good intel. We're asking your help with this. That's the reason for this meeting."

Tucker sensed that, by now, Wilson was feeling pretty bad. He'd never served on a SEAL Team before, didn't know how they operated and how easily feathers could get ruffled, especially when there was so much down time. He knew the men were trained, programmed to be ready to go. Boredom was one of their enemies. They were men of action.

He decided to talk to the young boat guy and give some encouragement he might appreciate. For that, he didn't need Kyle's permission. It was just helping out a fellow team member.

He glanced at Brawley, who sat next to Ollie Culbertson, his arms crossed on his chest and his gaze off to the side, which was worrisome.

"Here's the deal," Kyle continued. "Today, Jean and I and several others are going to drive up to Abeokuta, which is the local provincial capitol here. It's a fuckin' huge city of some half mil, a hub for the trans-Nigeria railroad that connects neighboring Chad, Niger, Cameroon to the west coast, Benin, and beyond."

"May I add something, Chief?" Jean requested.

Kyle stepped aside and motioned for him to take the floor again.

"There are things that happen up north in the capitol of the country, which is Abuja. But there are also business interests that flourish and enjoy being *outside* the capitol, especially with access to good transportation, the Gulf, and the Atlantic. Growing up, we always knew the multicultural aspect of our society was greatest at the coast, naturally, due to old trade routes and alliances. And believe me, there are those who appreciate being farther away from the politicians and their cronies." Jean turned and gave Kyle the floor. "Continue, Chief."

Tucker understood the dynamic they were talking about. If people wanted to conduct business without political interference, they'd do it as far away as possible, until their activities drew attention and brought them out of the shadows.

A trade in human trafficking or smuggling might be one of those businesses.

"We're going to send this in for analysis." Kyle held up the bundle and unwrapped the towel from the double bagged package, still frozen. "We believe this to be the hand of a young woman. And there is evidence part of a finger was removed, for some reason. It's common in ransom cases as a verification. It also scares the pants off loved ones and increases the size of the payout. But we're puzzled as to why the whole hand was removed and then discarded. And we're not sure if a subject could survive such a procedure if done out here in the jungle. So we're going to see what we can learn in town today."

"We'll take two trucks and two men with the boat crew. The rest of you will hang out here, ready, should we need you. You can use this time to contact your families, sleep, do PT, or watch some movies. You are to stay indoors, and as of today, you can use your cell phones. Right Jean?"

"It's set up. Yes. I have the passcodes posted in the lounge upstairs. Again, do not make your calls outside this building. And always safest to use the equipment here, which is hooked up to our satellite link."

"Questions?"

"How long will we be gone?" asked Ollie.

"Ollie, you're staying here. But the teams going north are the following: Cooper, Armando, Fredo, T.J., Rory, Jameson, Patrick, Danny, Jake, and Tucker.

DeWayne, you and one of Jean's guys will go with Wilson and Carson by boat. That leaves the six of you to yourselves, but you'll also have two of Jean's men guarding the perimeter."

"So how long, Chief?" Ollie asked again.

"We'll be back before dark. Anything else?"

"We pack light?" asked Armando.

"Leave your long guns here, Armani. Take your sidearms. You heard Jean yesterday. Never be without your sidearm."

The team was dismissed. Kyle shouted above the rumble of the crowd, "Leaving in thirty minutes."

Tucker waited for Brawley, but when he couldn't find him, he sought out young Wilson, pulling him into the hallway.

"What's up, Tucker?" the young Dine warrior asked.

"I just wanted you to know you're doing a great job. I'm so fuckin' impressed with you. You did good today. And if you wanted to crow a little bit about the adventure, well, everyone understands that's a newbie mistake. Not anything serious."

"Yea, I only told Danny and one other guy—"

"I get it. And Danny should have told you so, but keep your mouth shut until you're asked. Just don't offer. All new guys go through this. You want to make a good impression. Don't worry about it, kid. In no time, someone else will be new, and you get to help them."

"Thanks, Tuck. I appreciate that."

"I still got the same things going on, Wilson, and I'm an old fart. But I'm still new to this rotation, because the Navy changes, the Teams change. We're doing things way different than even ten years ago."

"Thanks, man." He fist-bumped Tucker.

"No problem. And remember, they look like big tough guys, but they're really pussies at heart."

Wilson had a deep chuckle over that one.

"Gotta split."

Tucker took the stairs two at a time to their second-floor room to gather his gear.

He checked his medic kit and double-checked his clips. He slipped his Kevlar vest over his long-sleeved tee shirt. Like most of the other Team guys, he'd customized the Velcro pockets that held his smaller gear. He was applying a repellant towelette to his neck, face, feet, and lower arms when he heard Brawley walk in.

He raised his head just in time to see Brawley head straight for him. When his buddy's palms smacked flat against his upper torso, Brawley pushed Tucker into the adjacent wall.

"What the fuck was that, Tucker?"

If it wasn't Brawley, Tucker would have immediate-

ly answered the assault and with lethal force, if necessary. But it was *Brawley*. The guy who'd been there for
him his whole life. The guy who'd suffered and was not
quite fully recovered. Tucker stuffed down his anger
and responded in a cool, measured tone.

"You fucking get your hands off me, Brawley. Get
your shit together, and then we can talk." He held his
arms to the side, which he hoped Brawley would see as
a submissive move. He made sure the eye contact was
anything but.

Brawley bunched up a couple of his vest flaps, curl-
ing his fingers, then pushed off Tucker, and swore
under his breath.

"You wanna tell me what's going on?" he asked
Brawley. He was hoping the choice would be made to
keep their interaction from escalating. "Talk to me,
Brawley," he nudged further.

Tucker could hear several other guys gathering
downstairs. Someone was playing some rock-n-roll,
mentally gearing up for the mission. He hoped Brawley
got that he was trusting him to make the right choice.
It was clearly up to him now.

"You said something to Kyle," Brawley barked
through his teeth, not making eye contact.

"And told him what? I've barely talked to Kyle
since yesterday. What the hell do you mean?"

"Is there a reason why I'm not going on the trip to

the city?"

"Fuck, Brawley, there are six of you not going! I don't think anyone else feels that way. Your time will come." It was obvious Brawley was short on the emotional reserves. In the old days, he'd have never thought of it this way.

"How'd you get favored treatment, Tucker? You tattling to the chief?"

"Is there something I should be telling him? You ask yourself that right now, Brawley, because you're bordering on some psycho shit. Now get your head out of your ass and wake up. You can't be prepared when you have all this garbage floating around in your head."

Brawley looked away, deep in thought.

Tucker extended an olive branch. He touched his shoulder and squeezed. "Get some rest, man. Perfect time to get caught up. And stay off the booze. Next time I smell it on you, I will tell Kyle. Don't make me do that."

Brawley nodded solemnly.

"Remember, it's not about you. It's the *other* guy. He deserves you at one hundred percent. You owe that to the Team."

"You're right, you fuckin' asshole." After a tense couple of seconds, Brawley followed it up with a wide grin.

"You forget your meds?"

"Didn't take the one last night. It was an oversight."

"Another reason to stay completely sober. Brawley, you gotta get turned around about all this. Talk to me tonight if you need to. We gotta handle this shit right now. I love you, man, and don't want to see anything happen you'll regret."

They embraced quickly, following it up with a pat on the back, then separated.

"Hooyah," Brawley whispered.

As Tucker ran down the stairs to the waiting group in the reception area, he knew it was only a matter of time before he was going to have to make a major intervention. He'd give Brawley one last chance. And if it didn't improve, he'd make sure he got declared medical and would get Kyle to ship him home. He was kicking himself at the decision made to allow Brawley back on the team.

His best friend was still not whole. Tucker vowed Brawley's condition wouldn't cause anyone else on the team to suffer. This was on him, and it was up to him to make sure everyone else was safe. Tucker knew it was his responsibility to protect the Team.

He knew he could fix it.

DEWAYNE AND THE three others gingerly carried the raft to the water and took off. The rest of the team loaded their bags into the two vehicles and began their trip to the rendezvous point designated. Tucker's last sight of their compound was through the rear window of the rover he was in, watching Brawley, Ollie, and others standing inside the compound gates with their hands in their pockets. Just before they disappeared from view, he watched Ollie give Brawley a backward kick to the butt, sending him to the ground.

They wound through the dense foliage on the dirt trail, passing trading posts, clusters of huts, and one make-shift school which had not been repaired from a recent fire that had engulfed one of the classrooms on the end. There were several children playing in the yard, but the school appeared to be closed.

The trail crossed a two-lane paved road, traffic going in both directions and congested with a variety of small trucks filled with people riding in the bed and seated on the side rails, busses and scooters. Leone skillfully blended into the flow of traffic behind the other vehicle. Though each direction had a single lane, in most cases, three vehicles occupied that spot, jockeying for position and avoiding contact.

In the minutes that followed, more and more commercial properties came into view. Bus stops with brightly colored advertising and gas stations started to appear. As they rounded a gradual turn to the left, they could at last see the huge city sprawling up the gentle slope, literally covering the entire landscape. Spires of churches were prevalent, as well as several prayer towers and domes. As they entered the city proper, the traffic came to nearly a standstill. Along the side of the road were sellers of various wares, including water bottles. Once, when they were stopped, a small boy tried to sell Tucker a baby crocodile no longer than a foot, its mouth secured shut with a rubber band.

Chickens dodged cars, carts, and bicycles. Dogs slept in doorways and under concrete benches. Tucker also noticed rows of unemployed men sitting on their haunches, watching the noisy procession in front of them.

The temperature of the city was cooler than where their bunker was. Most of the larger buildings were covered in red clay tiles, but smaller single-story structures like homes and shops were covered in rusty corrugated metal, patched and repaired numerous times. The roofline looked like a colorful patchwork quilt. Here and there, a large banyan-like tree arched above the buildings, but in general, there was very little landscaping.

Leone followed the Areva Afrique truck ahead as it turned west and headed toward their planned meeting point. Tucker read several signs directing tourists to Nigerian museums, frequently dedicated showing off artifacts of the slave trade. A large customs house was located a block away from the river bank, the area surrounding it paved with brick, making it a huge open-air marketplace filled with vendors stalls. A painted green and white sign on the building indicated it was the old slave marketplace, with a date chiseled in a stone block below it of 1502. Beneath that were the words *Point Of No Return.*

The vehicles pulled to a stop while Leone gave out instructions. "Follow Jean through the marketplace. We have a few minutes before the boat guys should arrive, so feel free to wander but not too far. Stay in groups of at least three."

"Can we use our dollars?" Tucker asked.

"They love dollars. That's more than a day's salary, but show your money cautiously, and be very careful about pickpockets. The locals don't figure it's illegal to cheat or steal from you. Do not use any of the cash machines, if you can find them, and don't exchange your money at a Chinese trader."

Danny asked for the exchange rate.

"I think roughly three hundred sixty Naira to the dollar."

"So where do we meet up?" asked Tucker.

Leone pointed to a small gate next to the custom house. "We'll be meeting them as they come through there. We have a place where we can leave the boat undisturbed, and Obe will guard it. You can leave your bags in the vehicle for me to guard. Be at the gate no later than,"—he checked his watch—"eleven hundred. That would be about right."

Tucker's group stuck together as they wandered through the marketplace. There was a section that sold fish and meats and another that sold local vegetables and cheeses.

They came upon a stall selling handmade stringed instruments of all sizes that attracted Jameson's attention. He drew quite a crowd when he pulled down a long stringed instrument looking like a banjo, consisting of stretched skin over a calabash, and tried to play it. The neck on the instrument was nearly a foot longer than a classical banjo, and it had only three strings. The owner asked Jameson if he wanted a demonstration.

The musician began a series of repeating refrains varying slightly in syncopation but keeping to the same time. With that background, the musician chanted, his voice picking up notes in harmony to the stringed beat, cutting in and out at half-intervals similar to a blues performer. Several small children instantly appeared and started dancing in a circle at their feet, each one trying to outdo the other. Another shopkeeper picked up a thumb piano and joined in the song and dance.

Kyle's group heard the music and turned to see what the ruckus was all about. Tucker threw his arms to the side, and Kyle closed his eyes, shaking his head in disbelief.

As soon as the music stopped, several shopkeepers ran to the circle, pushing their instruments in Jameson's face, holding out their percussion bells, wooden xylophones, reed flutes, and animal skinned drums, as well as every size of stringed instrument imaginable. He was overwhelmed and overridden with vendors all wanting his dollars.

Tucker helped extricate him from the crowd, purchasing the thumb piano from the original vendor, which seemed like the only way to get Jameson free. The transaction cost him ten bucks.

They located Kyle's group very close to the gate and stayed focused on catching up. Several of the men stopped along the way and bought beaded bracelets sold by children but passed up the dried fish heads, snakes and mummified baby crocodiles.

Jean was on his phone and then approached Tucker.

"We have to return the specimen to my contact at the local Civil Guard, since it's an internal matter. I'm going to ask him some questions, and we'll go from there."

Tucker retrieved it from his backpack. The package was dripping and was starting to smell. He gingerly handed it over to Jean, who reluctantly took it.

The small Jeep-like vehicle with blue lights arrived and pulled some distance away as Jean ran over to meet him, clutching the package and letting it drip in his hand. Just then, DeWayne and the two boat guys came through the rusty gate to greet them.

"Uneventful trip?" Kyle asked.

"We had some traffic just before we came to the city limits. But the river looked pretty deserted today," said Carson.

"How'd you like the ride, DeWayne?" Tucker asked.

"Cool. Felt like I had become my daddy in Nam. It was a time warp," DeWayne answered.

Jean returned with news there had not been any kidnappings reported for nearly two weeks. But the policeman suggested they speak with the aid agencies and one of the pastors.

After their guide rinsed his hands in the fountain, he asked them to join him in a quick tour of the city.

They stayed to the main street, detouring down only a few side streets. Jean noted the police stations and the emergency pharmacies, letting them know what could be purchased there. He pointed out the government offices, most of them in their own separate, gated compounds. He recommended which restaurants to stay away from and which street vendors had food that would not make them sick.

He showed them the great houses of some of the civic leaders and which homes were owned by their own African-Bollywood celebrities and wealthy businessmen.

Kyle split them into two groups. Tucker was in the group that made the trek to the Baptist Foreign Mission Church, to speak to the new, young reverend. T.J. and several others went off in search of the Africa Corp Administration building.

Reverend Gordon Schusler was picking up bibles and hymnals left in the pews, being helped by a couple of young boys who chased up and down the rows of seats, dropping books and chattering with excitement.

Schusler looked like he was fresh out of seminary. Tucker noted a bulge under the back of the pastor's shirt, and assumed he was probably carrying a firearm.

"We're here on a humanitarian mission, assessing some electrical grid issues for Areva Afrique," Jean began. "We came across evidence of a campsite and discovered a severed body part."

The reverend turned pale. His eyes shifted nervously amongst the group.

"The local Civil Guard told us to check with you to see if you were aware of any disappearances, especially perhaps any white woman?"

The reverend quickly scanned his little chapel, swallowed hard, and appeared not to have hardened to the realities of the region. He checked the area behind him before he spoke.

"Oh, that pains me to hear. There is so much talk of violence now that the elections are coming up. But no, I'm not aware of anyone missing amongst our ex-pat community. But I can ask around on Sunday, if you like."

"Would you, please?"

"You hear any talk about active human trafficking groups lurking in the area?" Kyle asked him next.

"The locals trust me. We discuss many things," he said as he set the books on a table in the narthex. "I was just telling some of my colleagues in other regions that it appeared to be quieting some. I was hoping that perhaps the Civil Guard were doing a good job with apprehension." He shrugged. "But you never know here. These people could be members of my church. My understanding is they blend in very well with the local population."

Tucker could see fear written all over the young reverend's face.

"I know you're going to think I'm insane, but there was a rumor earlier in the year that a local dentist was conducting raids. One of the teachers recognized him. Can you believe that?"

Jean handed the clergyman his card. "Call me anytime if you hear of anything."

THEY REGROUPED AN hour later, the boat crew team

returning to the shore and the rest of the team heading for the vehicles. T.J. was quite animated with his discovery at the medical mission.

"They've got three new teams just arrived to do health evaluations and give vaccinations at the schools, which start back up in two days. They've had a national holiday."

"And?" asked Kyle.

"They've lost contact with one of the teams, who were supposed to check in day before yesterday."

Kyle and Jean shared a look.

"This is out of your jurisdiction, Kyle. We have to let the locals handle it, and I'll get my trusted friend on it. But it means we've stumbled onto one of the cells, I think. We're close."

CHAPTER 14

BRANDY GOT THE call from Tucker just before she was leaving for work. His handsome face was such a welcomed sight.

"You look great, Tucker!"

He gave her a crooked smile and winked. "I could say the same. How are you doing, sweetheart?"

"I've been busy painting, spending some time with Dorie and Jessica, and had lunch with Libby Brownlee. And of course, there's Dad with his schoolboy crush."

He chuckled. "I can only imagine what that's like. He probably feels like he's starting over."

"At first, I think he wanted to hold back, you know, because of my mother. Now, well, I finally had to take a couple of days off he was getting to me so much."

"Ah, let him have his fun."

"So how have you been? Anything interesting you can tell me?" she asked.

He rolled his eyes. "Nope. But I'll have lots of stories when I get home. Very different over here. I spent most of my time in Iraq and Afghanistan before, so this is a change in one way and not so much in others."

His voice quieted and Brandy sensed he wasn't anxious to go into detail, even if he could.

"You staying safe?"

"I think so. We're in a pretty good spot. Oh, and you'll love this. We went into the market today, and I bought some trinkets, but you should have seen the instruments. They have this long banjo-looking three-stringed thing that Jameson loved. Course, he couldn't play it worth a damn, so we got a little concert from the shopkeeper. The kids were dancing all around us. A real Sound of Music moment. You would have loved it."

"That's totally not what I expected! So did he buy the banjo?"

"Nope. Way too big to lug that thing home. But I bought him what's called a finger piano. It's got—well, next call I'll get it out for you. You can search the internet too. There is a metal plate carved into fingers that are different lengths. The whole piece is nailed to a wooden bowl, and they use soda pop bottle lids to hold it in place. Very different and makes a beautiful sound. He's driving us all crazy with it."

"Sounds cool. Is the weather okay?"

"Muggy. Bugs. Dusty. I'm sure you get the picture."

"How do you feel being back in the Scouts?" She knew he'd pick up on the code word for Teams.

Tucker shrugged. "Work is work. Some fact finding today. Got a tour of the city, visited a little mission chapel, saw some unbelievable houses owned by the wealthy, too. It's just different. Lots of lucky chickens and lazy dogs. Parts are incredibly beautiful, and then there are other parts that break your heart."

Brandy saw a wrinkle develop on his forehead.

"How's Brawley doing?"

"Fine. He's doing fine."

Tucker's smile was flat. Fine was not a word he used very often, and Brandy sensed there was something deeper behind it.

"Have you eaten any of the local food?"

"We have a cook, if you can believe it. He's made some tasty stuff. They use coconut yams and peppers in everything. Make a red and green curry-like sauce and eat it over rice or potatoes, like a chutney. A lot of seafood. Some of it reminds me of Cajun food, like jambalaya. There's this red oil that takes your breath away. So far so good. Not had any stomach issues yet, but it's early."

"How long will you be, or do you know?" she asked.

"We're just getting started, really. I can't say, even if I knew." Tucker turned around to speak to someone.

"Hey, we got another line tonight, so I need to sign off soon."

"No problem. I'm thrilled we got to talk. Always makes me feel better when I can see your face. So glad we get to do that."

"Me too. I've been writing in the journal you packed for me. Kind of my evening routine before bedtime. Wish I could write a letter, but you'll get caught up when I bring it home."

"Can't wait. Well, you take good care of yourself. I'm proud of you, Tucker. They're lucky to have you. Just remember what you promised."

"I think of that all the time. I'll be home before you know it. I really appreciate being able to see a little bit of home. Not enough, of course, but it will tide me over for now."

She kissed her phone screen. Tucker gave her the peace sign and disconnected.

She was left standing in her living room, her body shaking. She hoped they'd have longer next time, and she kicked herself for not asking when he'd be contacting her again. But she was grateful for the call. She sensed he was covering a little for Brawley but knew better than to get a report over the phone.

It was just good to hear his voice, feel that connection.

After work, Brandy had made an appointment with

a personal trainer Dorie recommended. It was to be a trial, complimentary session. She met Cory in the equipment room. He was a much shorter and more compact version of Tucker, and he eagerly showed her a routine she could follow, marking machines and numbers of reps on a card he created for her. She wanted to show him how strong she was by pushing herself to the limits of exhaustion, though he cautioned to take it slower.

"I want to have guns like yours by the time my husband comes back," she announced.

Cory gave her a goofy scrunched up expression and responded, "Doesn't work that way, Brandy. Just be consistent. You don't have to push yourself, experience all that pain. Besides, if you do that, you won't enjoy it."

She went ahead and booked another three trainings at their introductory discounted price and was feeling really good about concentrating on her health. She could also feel the effects of her exertions and knew she'd be a little sore tomorrow, but put it out of her mind.

Instead of going home to a heavy dinner or eating fast food, she sat in the juice bar and ordered a healthy green drink that was gritty and tasted terrible. She was about to dump it and leave for home when three of Dorie's bridesmaids walked into the spa, dressed in their designer workout sets, complete with headbands and fancy shoes she knew cost hundreds of dollars.

The ladies attracted quite a bit of attention as they sauntered through the lobby. Marsha, the one who was married to a Team 5 guy, recognized her and came bounding up to say hello, her perky ponytail flapping behind her like a school girl.

"Brandy? Is that really you?"

The initial blast of Marsha's perfume made Brandy's eyes water. She drew down a large slurp of the green drink, trying to look as if she was enjoying it, before she answered. "Oh hi. You're Marsha, is that right?"

"Come on over here, girls. You remember Brandy? From Dorie's wedding?"

The other two floated to Marsha's side. "Who could forget that wedding?" one of them said.

"And I'm so glad we finally got that bustier on you, Brandy. How embarrassing it would have been if we'd torn the material or we couldn't get it on," the other girl said.

"That would have been a good America's Funniest Videos, for sure," answered Marsha.

Brandy wanted to throw the drink in her face. Instead, she laughed at herself with the rest of them and slurped. The seaweed and grass something-or-other drink was starting to grow on her and didn't taste as bad the third time.

"So how is Dorie? We haven't seen her here in ages," Marsha asked.

"Jessica takes up a lot of her time now that she's walking."

The other two squealed their O.M.G.s and surprise that they'd had a baby. "I'll bet Brawley is a *divine* dad," said one of them.

Brandy wanted them to just go away and leave her alone. But she was surrounded by other people, including her new personal trainer. "How's married life treating you, Marsha?" Brandy figured that would be mean enough.

"Gone." She held up her bare ring finger.

Brandy wasn't surprised. She wrapped her fingers around her straw, taking another sip and showing off her very small diamond. But it was a diamond given to her by a man who truly loved her just the way she was.

"Brandy!" Marsha whispered. "When did you get married?"

"About two years ago now. Met him at Dorie's wedding."

"You married a Team guy?" one of the girls remarked.

"Yes. Tucker, Brawley's best friend. You remember him, don't you?"

"The one who held your hair back while you were

throwing up? That was so sweet of him, Brandy," Marsha said with a sad, long face.

"Yes, that was very touching. We all watched. Such a sweetheart!" said another.

Brandy's nails dug into the Styrofoam cup. She took another long pull, which made a loud slurping sound when she hit bottom.

"Well," Brandy began. "I just finished my workout with Cory, and I'm off. Hope to see you here again, ladies."

The three friends gave her a hug, one by one, and then disappeared into the women's locker room. Brandy tossed her cup, swung her bag over her shoulder, and headed for her car. She knew she was angry and wished she had the courage to go all Ta-Wanda on one of their cars. But she closed her eyes and thought about the life she had now.

She was the lucky one.

CHAPTER 15

THE TEAM SORTIES began to pay off. Several sightings were made of a group of men who had traveled from the north. There had been a recent skirmish, and several villagers had been killed after the Africa Corp caught a similar band of men trying to abduct a classroom full of young girls. Reverend Schusler had an older member of his congregation he wanted the men to interview.

Brawley had been chosen to accompany Tucker and a small group, including Danny and DeWayne, to interview her. Kyle and Jean were off to a meeting with the Civil Guard. Ollie and several others were sent to visit the school that had been fire damaged, since school had re-started in the region. T.J. and Coop visited the aid workers office to see if they'd made contact with their missing team. All the groups had a man from Jean's team accompany them and were to assemble at noon near the river.

Reverend Schusler introduced his parishioner to Tucker and the others. DeWayne helped with the translation. She spoke French but little English. De-Wayne had studied Yoruba.

"She has a granddaughter who has gone missing," Reverend Schusler said in a whisper.

DeWayne gave an introduction, first in French and then shifted to her native Yoruba and got better results.

She was animated, rocking back and forth as she sat in the pew, then waving her arms as she spoke. Tucker could see DeWayne was having a little difficulty at first understanding her dialect.

"She says her granddaughter works for one of the big houses, I assume those are the houses on the hill, as a houseworker," translated DeWayne. He stopped to listen further and then added, "She says sometimes that does involve a little sex, as her granddaughter is a pretty girl."

Brawley tensed, and Tucker knew he was stuffing down some choice words.

"Unfortunately, this is common," added Reverend Schusler.

"Do you know who she works for?" Tucker asked.

"No, but I can have her show me later, if you want." Reverend Schusler patted the woman's shoulder and spoke gently to her in French, encouraging her to continue speaking.

Tucker's stomach boiled. "How old is she?"

Dewayne waited for the answer back. "Fifteen," he said, his eyes downcast.

Brawley's eyes were red with anger. Tucker felt the same way. They listened to the woman tell the rest of her story. She drew a cloth from her bodice and wiped her eyes as she began to sob.

DeWayne paused. "Her daughter was kidnapped several years ago, and since then, she's been raising her two granddaughters. This one is the youngest. The older one was able to go to a boarding school in England sponsored by the mission."

Schusler nodded. "Yes, yes. Bimi. Very bright. She's doing well, we hear." He hesitated, "So she is Bimi's little sister? I don't recall seeing her at church."

Dewayne asked the grandmother about that. "She says Sunday is the only day she has to sleep. She works very hard, very long hours for the big man. It was on Sunday she went missing. At first, she thought she'd been called to work, but when they sent a messenger around on Monday when she didn't show up, her grandmother knew something was wrong."

Tucker asked Dewayne to translate. "Your grand-daughter, does she attend school?"

The woman shook her head.

"So she's been gone how many days?"

She held up two fingers.

"When was the last time she saw her?"

DeWayne came back with the answer. "She was asleep when she left for church Sunday morning."

"Ask her if she has a picture of her," Tucker instructed.

The answer came back, "No."

Reverend Schusler spoke to the woman in French again. He listened and translated her answer. "She says she doesn't think her big boss has anything to do with her disappearance."

"Do you believe her?" asked Tucker.

"I do."

"Ask her to show us to the house. We can drive her there. We'd like to ask her employer some questions."

As the Reverend spoke, the woman got agitated and refused, shaking her head. She continued explaining something in Yoruba.

DeWayne gave them her answer. "She says she can point to it. You can see it from the front steps of the chapel. But she says she will not go there, because she does not want to offend the big man."

Tucker thanked the Reverend and shook the grandmother's hand. *"Merci, madame,"* he said over and over again, as he bowed to her.

She led them to the street, faced the rise in the distance, and pointed to a bright pink house with lots of vines covering the outside. It was one of the largest ones in the neighborhood.

"Do you know this person, pastor?" asked Brawley.

"No. Probably a foreigner. Could be a local official. Your friend Jean might know who he is, but I don't. My flock isn't from there," he said and then turned back inside the chapel.

Tucker took a picture of the house with his cell phone camera. They headed to their rendezvous point to report their findings.

Kyle and Jean were waiting for them. When Tucker showed Jean the picture of the house, he was rewarded with an answer.

"Dutch businessman. Makes cell phones and electronic components. He's white. He doesn't fit the profile."

"So the Civil Guard will interview him, then?" said Kyle.

"That would be best. I'll get someone over there now." He was walking away, talking on his cell as Ollie and his group returned.

"Anything at the school?" Tucker asked Ollie.

"We talked to a couple of the teachers. Everything so far has been normal," said Ollie. "No one missing, no one hanging around, and they haven't seen anything unusual. But we gave them Jean's card."

"What about the fire?" asked Kyle.

"They attributed the fire to a faulty extension

cord."

T.J. and Coop were jogging toward them. Tucker knew they'd found something.

"Any word?" Kyle asked.

"They're MIA," answered Coop, catching his breath.

T.J. added, "They get their supplies in those plastic bins, like what Tucker brought back. I have a gut feeling our girl was from that team." He handed a sheet of paper to Kyle, still gasping for breath. "Here are the details of the missing aid workers. We got three women and four men."

Kyle took the paper and began scanning. His face grew pale as he stared back at T.J. "One of these is American."

CHAPTER 16

KYLE OBTAINED VERIFICATION from the State Department that Sheila Coburn was indeed a twenty-three-year-old nurse from California. The Africa Doctors' Corps had inserted three new teams after finishing their training in France. They were to work primarily with children in the schools, since they could perform their examinations and vaccinations easily without having to travel all over the bush. And it needed to be done before the school year got out. The hope was that they'd be on the front lines of any further Ebola outbreak, as had occurred in the DRC.

Back at the bunker, they received a photograph of the young nurse, as well as pictures of the other six members of her team. The two other women were from Belgium. One was a nurse and the other a doctor who had been working off and on in Africa for nearly ten years. Two of the men were from Italy, one from Norway, and another from Algeria. The medic from

Norway had served in the Special Forces. This was his first humanitarian gig.

Tucker eyed the picture of Sven Tolar with his intense cool blue eyes. He'd served in Afghanistan with several Norwegian SO troops, and he had high regard for their abilities.

"If this man's still alive, he'll be a huge asset for us," he said.

"I agree," said Jean.

"So this changes things," started Kyle. "State's made the request, and the SOF Africa Command has given us authorization to do a rescue or recovery. There are other embassy personnel in the region here for a conference, but at present, we don't think they're in danger. So our main goal is to locate and return these aid workers safely, by lethal force, if necessary."

Tucker knew that the other SEALs were as excited as he was about finally getting their hands dirty. He knew no one outside the community could ever understand that.

"We're getting some satellite infrared feeds after sunset. Once we locate the group, we'll launch. So get locked and loaded, get some sleep, check your bags and be ready when we get the call." Kyle turned to Jean. "Anything else you want to say?"

Jean studied the hostage pictures before he turned them over to Cooper. "My guys don't have identification yet on the hand, but I wouldn't hold my breath from the Civil Guard. At this point, we should assume we have a severely injured female and six traumatized hostages. Good news is that we have a combat medic and a doctor in this group. That bodes well."

It wasn't great news, but Tucker decided he'd take it.

After the team was dismissed, Wilson approached Kyle. "Sir, are we a go?"

"Depends on where we have to get to. We will leave a few men behind here, and who knows, maybe you'll have to come rescue us?" Kyle grinned.

Wilson and Carson tore upstairs. Tucker was right behind them.

Brawley had showered and was quickly getting dressed and gearing up. "It's showtime, Tuck. Didn't come all this way to spend my afternoons at the bazaar."

"Roger that. I'm going to shower, and then I'd like to get some shuteye. You okay with that?"

"No complaints here."

Tucker quickly cleaned up, rinsed out his shirt from today's trip, and hung it with the pants he'd washed earlier over the chair in their room. He finished getting fully dressed, including his vest and his boots with doubled up socks. He lay down, Brawley serenading him with his snoring. Just before he fell asleep, he heard the faint tune from Jameson's finger piano. He knew that from now on, every time he heard that sound, he'd think of this moment, getting ready to hopefully save the day.

BRAWLEY BARKED IN his ear, waking him from a sound sleep. "It's a go. Get up, Tucker."

The sky was black. He followed Brawley to the lounge and then down the stairs to where the rest of the team waited.

Kyle had sheets of paper spread over the countertop in the kitchen. "Help yourselves, and then take a seat." He pointed to the large tub that held bottled waters. Next to it was a box of energy bars, nut packets, and meal replacement shakes.

"Our satellite images show they've been moving around in a circular fashion." He showed the clip that had been downloaded to him earlier. "We're here."

Several men swore.

"Yeah, they're close, really close, and probably heading our way. So we're leaving a small force here at the bunker with the Zodiac. They've stopped moving, so we're guessing they've bedded down for the night. Jean and his guys are going to get ahead of them in case they run back to the city. The rest of us are going to meet them on the road. Going to spread out in three teams. We have to stop them before they get to the river," said Kyle. "And we don't have any time to coordinate local help, but the Civil Guard have been notified. We're on our own."

Kyle demonstrated the route they'd be taking on the map. "Wear your night vision, of course, and we're going to take our Invisios. I'll give a com to each team. Coop, you lead one. I'll get one, and, Tucker, I'd like you to lead the other."

It hit Tucker in the gut that he'd been given a lead the first time out. He chanced a glance to Brawley, whose nod was nearly imperceptible.

"Snipers take your long guns, and Fredo, you and your guys make sure you load up on percussive and flash devices. Once we get a count, all three teams will hit at once, after Fredo tosses the percussive blast."

He called out the teams and the men staying behind with Wilson and Carson. He handed Tucker the sat phone, which he attached to his vest in the Velcro pocket he'd made especially for that purpose. Fredo passed out the Invisios so the team leaders could communicate.

Two of Jean's men were dressed in black sniper gear to guard the compound from the outside, with one man on the roof. The gate was opened, and the three teams jogged into the night, following the road. Jean's men left in one of the Rovers.

Along the way, Tucker's NV picked up the reflective gold eyes of small animals in the brush.

When they arrived at the launch point, they assembled one last time to coordinate the strike. Kyle's tablet showed the latest heat signatures of more than a dozen people clustered in groups. It was impossible to make an accurate count. None of the images were moving. He motioned for Tucker to take his group, which included Ollie and Brawley around to the right, sending Coop to the west, on the left side of the encampment. Kyle would attack the middle.

"We are a go." said Kyle. "Check in, and wait for my mark."

Tucker's group was able to follow a trail for several hundred feet and then came upon the campsite. A bright blaze from the campfire temporarily obscured his night vision, so he turned it off and flipped the scope up out of the way. His eyes slowly adjusted until he could see the sleeping forms ahead.

"We're in place," he whispered and heard the confirmation from Coop and Kyle.

"We can't get a count," said Kyle. "Tucker?"

"Checking now," he returned. Tucker moved closer. The fire gave him good visual advantage. He made out three forms tied together surrounding a small tree. They all appeared to be males. Another form sat in the driver's seat of an older Jeep-type vehicle, a rifle of some kind lay across his lap. He appeared to be the lookout, but his head dropped, and Tucker determined he was asleep.

"Got three males tied together right, sentry asleep in the Jeep, armed." He inched closer. "Troop convoy has no movement but can't see the back. We have eight, no, nine sleeping forms on the ground. I can't see the women."

"Shit."

Tucker froze, holding Brawley from moving forward.

"That's two unaccounted for," whispered Kyle. "Armani, anything?"

"I got eleven on the ground."

"On my mark. Three...two..."

Tucker waited, breathing slow. Then someone stumbled right over the top of them, coming from behind. As he fell, the man fired and woke up the whole camp. Fredo's blast went off simultaneously.

Tucker heard a thump and thought perhaps he'd been hit, but he remembered he'd worn his Kevlar. Brawley hit the shooter once in the head, the dark spray indicating it was a kill shot. Rounds started flying toward them, scraping the ground, tearing apart leaves, and pinning them down. "One kill," he whispered into his mic.

Cooper's team hit the group from cover behind the vehicles. The sleeping driver had been taken out, but two panicked shooters started spraying the whole perimeter.

"Two," he heard in Coop's distinctive voice.

Tucker knew it would be nearly impossible for the automatic fire not to have hit someone on their team. There wasn't any cover, and they'd planned for a coordinated stealth hit on the whole group. Gunfire ricocheted off the vehicles, sending sparks flying. "Three, four," he heard, and the automatic spray in front of him was still.

He had to extinguish the fire so the team could use their night vision scopes. He hoped Brawley would cover him as he ran into the circle, grabbed a blanket which had been covering a bloody body, and threw it over the fire, stomping it down until there was darkness again. He felt a sting on his upper right arm, which spun him around. He dropped to his belly again, firing in the direction of the shooter, and heard him hit the ground. "Five," he whispered hoarsely.

Tucker repositioned his scope and noted the body next to him had a heat signature. He touched the face and knew it to be a woman. She groaned. "One woman hostage, alive but wounded."

From behind, Brawley cut down a dark form he'd missed, running straight for him. "Six," he reported.

They heard a woman's scream then a single shot. "Seven," said Armando.

"Eight and Nine," he heard Kyle count off.

"Danny's got ten," said Coop.

Tucker heard movement near where the three men had been tied up. He saw the outline of a man using them for cover, as they stomped their feet and tried to scream through gags. Before he could take aim, Ollie came up behind and slit the man's throat.

"Eleven."

Everything was silent until he heard Kyle's voice over the com. "Gather the wounded. Lights on."

Tucker flipped up his scope just in time before the high intensity lantern illuminated the scene. Coop and T.J. checked for signs of life and re-confirmed the body count. Brawley scanned the perimeter.

Tucker knelt by the wounded woman and was aghast that she was still alive. Her body shook from a raging fever. Her right arm was bandaged where it ended at the wrist and was soaked with blood. She had multiple other wounds on her legs and around her neck. Barely conscious, he brushed the hair from her face and checked her pulse, which was weak, but she was still alive.

"Hang in there. We got you. We're bringing you home," he whispered. She said something in French he couldn't understand.

"Got one of the Belgium girls," he barked. "Serious. Gonna need immediate attention."

Brawley cut through the binding on the three men and reported, "Kyle, they say there are only three. One lost, and they lost one of the girls, too."

He could hear the American girl talking fast in English, crying between her words. Ollie went over to her and helped her walk.

"I got you, sweetheart. Just lean on me." He kept her at the outside, helping her to sit on a boulder as she clung to him, sobbing into his upper thigh. "No worries. You're safe now."

The three aid workers raced over and began to help the Belgium woman. Tucker dropped his bag and handed them his medic kit. They worked with skill, giving her an injection of antibiotics and had the dressing changed in seconds. Those cool blue eyes stared up at him, but this time, they were smiling.

"Thank God you came when you did. She would have been dead by morning," he said in his Scandinavian accent.

Tucker answered him. "Nice to meet you, Sven."

"Jean? You guys out there?" Kyle barked without getting an answer. "Jean, we got eleven dead. We're going back with three males, a seriously injured female, and the American nurse relatively unharmed. We've been told the other two perished."

Tucker saw Kyle double checking the sat phone, swearing as he still didn't receive an answer.

Danny, Coop, Brawley, and others checked for I.D.s, notes, or maps from the dead and presented Kyle with a very sparse pile of papers. Kyle tucked them into his jacket.

"We can't wait any longer," whispered their chief into his Invisio. "Let's get everyone and the firearms in the lorry. Coop, can you get these puppies started?" Kyle said, pointing to the two vehicles.

"I'm on it," said the big SEAL, running.

Before anyone could move, a twelfth shooter appeared around the back of the troop transport, drilled a shot to the back of Ollie's head, grabbed the American nurse from behind, and screamed, "I'll shoot her!" He aimed his pistol under her chin, hauling her into the tiny Jeep while using her as a shield.

The Team was temporarily stunned as they watched the body of their brother slumped against the transport. As the sound of the open-air Jeep took off into the night, the distinctive crack of Armando's sniper rifle fired after him, but the Jeep continued.

Ollie's body pitched and fell to the ground like a limp rag.

CHAPTER 17

B RANDY WAS HEADED to the gym when Christy Lansdowne's number came up on the car's dash as an incoming call. Her heart immediately began to pound in her chest. Her hands got sweaty. She temporarily couldn't find the answer button and almost disconnected the call. Her mouth was parched.

"Christy?" she rasped.

"Hey, Brandy. There's been some trouble, and I wanted you to hear about it from me first before you see it on the news."

"Is Tucker—?"

"We have one fatality, but it isn't Tucker."

"Who?"

"I'm not allowed to say, but please don't breathe a word to anyone. Stay off your phone but have it by your side. More to come."

"You need help calling people?" Brandy asked, relieved that at least Tucker was alive.

"Oh thanks, sweetie, but I got this. I gotta run, but stay off the phone, and if anyone on the outside tries to contact you for details, you haven't heard anything. Understood?"

"Yes, ma'am. Thank you."

Brandy pulled over to the side of the road as hot tears slipped down her cheeks. Still in shock, she took several huge gulps of air to calm her nerves. But just when she was getting control of herself, a wave of pain flooded over her, and she lost it again. The proximity to danger, to the fact that Tucker could have been killed, had knocked her so hard, she was reeling from the aftermath, gasping to wrap her mind around it.

What does all this mean? Is he alive but injured in some way?

After regaining her composure, she turned her car around and headed home.

First thing that hit her was that the place looked so empty without Tucker there. Everything was the same as she'd left it, but now she saw it through a different set of eyes. She was desperate for information.

Who is it? Brawley?

She wanted to call Dorie but turned on the TV instead and sat watching the news, clutching her cell. She flipped the channels, hoping for some commentary on trouble in Africa. After nearly an hour, one of the stations finally broke for a special report that Special

Forces had been engaged in an altercation in an unknown location in Central Africa and that there were multiple fatalities.

Multiple fatalities?

Could Christy have not gotten the latest news? Were more members of the team injured—or…? She had to stop herself.

She ran to the kitchen and poured herself a tumbler of Tucker's whiskey, feeling it burn all the way down her throat. As she flipped from station to station, there wasn't any further detail.

HER CELL PHONE rang, waking her up. She'd fallen asleep on the couch, the glass tumbler was on its side in her lap, the TV still blaring in the background. The room was dark as the sun had set hours ago. She didn't want to look at the caller I.D. before answering.

"Hello?"

"Brandy. It's Dorie. I just needed to call someone. Did you—?"

"Is Brawley okay?"

"Yes. Tucker?"

"Yes, thank God."

She heard Dorie collapse on the other end of the phone. "I know I wasn't supposed to call. Please forgive me."

"Nonsense, Dorie. You want me to come over

while we wait?"

"Could you? Jessica is down for the night, but I could sure use some company."

"Be right over. You need me to bring anything?" Brandy asked.

"No, I'm good. Just come."

BRANDY WAS AT Brawley and Dorie's house in twenty minutes. She turned off her car radio, annoyed at the news hypes and all the advertising. The clock said one A.M when she arrived.

She knocked at the front door but let herself in without waiting. Dorie ran straight to her, wearing a long nightgown, and collapsed in her arms. Brandy immediately felt comforted wrapped in the arms of her best friend. Dorie's body was shaking in compulsive sobbing she couldn't contain. As she held Dorie, images of their years of friendship passed by her eyes as she relived and recounted all the happy days, all the big joys and trials they'd shared together, and prayed for a happy ending.

This cannot be!

"Come on. Let's sit. Have you tried watching the news?" Dorie's eyes were puffy, a vein in her forehead pulsed, and her chest heaved as she tried to get her breath.

"I—I haven't been able to find out anything, but I

stopped watching. I just couldn't."

Brandy understood how she felt.

"Well, we've heard both Tucker and Brawley are okay, so let's be grateful for what we know and pray for the families of all the others."

It broke her heart to think of the bonfire on their last weekend, all the wives and kids sitting around together. She finally understood why that was so important. Someone would get some bad news tonight—something she never wanted to hear.

As if she could will it so, she pushed all those thoughts out of her mind. Dorie lay curled up against her as she pulled a throw over both of them, and they held each other.

This was unknown territory for Brandy. Brushing the hair from Dorie's forehead, she tried to think of something that would soothe her.

"At least this time he's not missing like the last deployment. It sounds like they are safe. Just remember, Brawley isn't missing. He's coming home."

"Yes. This is different, but, Brandy, he had to work so hard to come back. It took him all that time in rehab. What's going to happen now?"

Brandy didn't have any answers for her but tried. "You know him, and you know he's strong. And this time, Tucker's with him. He also has you and Jessica. It's a whole new family he comes back to. He did it before. He can do it again."

After searching the news outlets again, they decided to go back to bed and wait out the word. Brandy left a message on her dad's cell so he wouldn't expect her for work and promised to get back.

Dorie insisted she stay over and offered her the bedroom, but Brandy needed to be on her own.

"Go take a shower, Dorie. It will relax you. And then turn in. I'll just borrow a pillow and sleep in the couch in front."

"Thank you. I have to get stronger about all this, or I won't survive."

"You don't say things like that, Dorie. You've got the baby and Jessica now to take care of too. He's going to need all the strength you can muster. I know you can do it."

"You're such a good friend, Brandy."

They hugged and retired for the night.

MORNING LIGHT HIT her across the face as her cell rang. It was Tucker!

"Tucker! Oh my God. Are you okay?"

"I'm fine."

There was that word again. She waited for further explanation.

"Um, we're coming home early. We lost a guy, and we're bringing him home."

"Christy told me. Who, Tucker?"

"Ollie Culbertson." Dead silence followed his whisper.

"I'm so sorry, Tucker. Are any of you injured at all?"

"Just a scratch. A few of us got banged up, but we're used to that. Just tough dealing with it. It will be good to get home. And, look, I can't stay on the line long. Just wanted you to hear it from me."

"Thank you. I've got you, Tucker. I'm going to dedicate myself to making you feel better."

He didn't answer back, which told Brandy there was much more he needed to say and couldn't. Then he whispered, "I'm not going to be very good company, Brandy. Just warning you. But I'll try."

"No worries. Don't even bother about that."

"And there's Brawley. He's a mess."

This was what she was expecting. "I understand. I'm at Dorie's house right now."

"Good. Listen, Kyle's going to call her, but don't mention that because she probably wants to hear from Brawley, so just tell her we're having to take turns here. And give her my best. I'll text you when I'm in country."

"Thank you, sweetheart. Love you, Tucker."

But he had disconnected the call.

CHAPTER 18

KYLE HAD MANAGED to get the Belgian doctor a medivac to the new trauma center at the capitol until she could be stabilized and then sent home to Belgium. The bird was to meet them back at the compound.

The decision was risky, but the Hajere Trauma Center was the closest available medical facility capable of handling her injuries. The capitol was about to become destabilized, and Sven and the other medics doubted she'd survive the trip back to Benin. It was hoped she'd be ready to be flown home to Belgium in two days' time.

The State Department confirmed that there was an impending coup about to break out any day and that Jean, through his contacts with the Civil Guard, had been detained until the SEALs were removed. There was worry that an armed government militia was on its way to prevent their leaving.

"Someone wants trophies," Cooper said.

"I'm guessing their timing was off, and they expected to intercept us on the way," said Kyle. "So, we have to get out of here immediately."

"Suits me fine. Can't wait to get out of this shithole," muttered Brawley. He wandered off into the dark, mumbling.

Everyone had to fit inside the only form of transportation they had: the one lorry. T.J. and Tucker wrapped Ollie's body in a blanket, securing it with rope, and loaded it on top of the canvas cover. Then they climbed up top with him. The doctor was laid out over the laps of four men in the second seat, and everyone else was jammed into the back. They also loaded up the weapons and tossed them in the back.

"Shit, where's Brawley?" asked Kyle.

"Goddammit," Tucker said as he jumped from the roof and switched on his light. "Brawley, where the fuck are you?"

Kyle chimed in. "Brawley? We gotta go? You want to wait for the bad guys?"

They heard someone across the firepit. Brawley was sitting cross-legged, rocking back and forth, mumbling something over and over again.

"I got him. Can I get some help?" Tucker shouted.

Several men hoisted him up, dumping him into the back. "Someone secure him if he tries to get out," Kyle barked.

They heard a "Roger that."

Brawley wasn't making any sense, and Tucker knew it was spooking the Team, but he could count on them to keep him restrained. Tucker jumped up top again, as the two others repositioned themselves and they headed out.

Cooper drove at break-neck speed, even though the night was still pitch black.

When they arrived at the compound, Jean's men had indeed pulled out, leaving the entire place unguarded. Wilson, Carson, and the other SEALs had convinced them to leave behind two of the four vehicles, which they had already packed, including the Zodiac and Wilson's precious engine.

Tucker was grateful they wouldn't have to hike out, especially now that they'd have to restrain Brawley and perhaps carry him.

The helicopter arrived and took charge of the doctor, as well as evacuated the two Italian workers. Sven Tolar agreed to accompany the SEAL Team to the Benin border and beyond to the coast where he could arrange transportation home.

"Before we head out, make sure you find your passports for the crossing. I don't want to fight our way back, if we don't have to."

Tucker had to find his in the bag that had been

thrown in the back of the Areva Afrique truck. He also found Brawley's.

"Everyone legal?" Kyle shouted. There were no complaints.

"I have mine as well," said Sven from the back.

Kyle eyed Tucker, leaning forward and giving quick glances to Brawley sitting between them. "Everything good?" Kyle asked.

"Perfect," returned Tucker. Brawley continued staring straight ahead, thankfully, without saying a word.

Several of the team had injuries, which Sven, T.J., and Cooper had treated, but nothing that couldn't wait until they got stateside. The idea was to cross the border at dawn and make it to Benin to catch a charter flight home. Tucker's job was to keep an eye on Brawley and keep him from wandering off.

The three trucks roared out of the compound and headed straight for what they hoped was the fastest route, the highway, since getting out stealth mode wasn't a priority. Cooper had DeWayne up front with him as a translator, while Kyle, Tucker and Brawley took the second seat. Sven sat behind. T.J. drove the second truck and Fredo the third.

They passed a convoy of military trucks heading north to the capitol, but the road otherwise was empty both ways.

Kyle ended his long call with his State Department liaison and shook his head.

"Sons of bitches said this caught them off guard. I'm not buying that," Kyle cursed.

"Excuse me, Chief Lansdowne," Sven inserted, "but we're always on alert here for potential coups. We have an election coming up in two weeks. You know how it works. If they think they're going to lose the election, they have a coup, and then there's a civil war. They couldn't have known for sure."

"Well, we were sent here to find the smugglers, not save the country."

"We did," said Coop. "We rescued four out of seven. If it was going to be easy, they'd have sent in somebody else."

Tucker agreed. But in the silence, he knew everyone was thinking about the man they lost.

TWO HOURS LATER, they'd raced through the crossing, which was oddly unmanned. The sky was growing pink as they traveled toward a coastal town, where State had made accomodations for them at a crumbling hotel.

Tucker snuck in his quick call to Brandy from his own cell to let her know he was coming home.

Relieved at least to have a bed and the possibility of some sleep, he felt more human. He laid Brawley back on his bed, removed his shoes, and gave him a shot so he'd sleep the night without wandering off. He suspected the PTSD diagnosis he'd had nearly two years ago had now flared up.

Sven stopped by to check in and say good-bye. They whispered so as not to disturb Brawley.

"Just wanted to say thanks. I was hoping I'd get to spend some time with you guys. Maybe take a raincheck?" His forehead was wrinkled as his eyebrows rose.

Tucker gave him a hug. "Not anytime soon."

"I understand," muttered Sven.

"I wanted to talk to you about your Spec Ops tour. We trained with some of you guys last gig, over ten years ago. And I served with a couple of your guys in Afghanistan. I got tons of respect, man."

"It's mutual."

"So how the hell did you get back here as an aid worker?"

Sven leaned against the doorframe, exhaled, and then began. "When I came home, there was no family left behind to welcome me back, and after I got out, I just couldn't focus. I tried applying for some private security, you know, contracting jobs. But when I read about the Doctors' Corp, I got inspired. I knew I could help protect the workers, and I wanted to give something back."

"See the other side of suffering and war."

"Exactly. I was saving lives overseas, but I just wanted to use my skills for good. This was my first one."

"And did it help?"

"I feel like the work's not finished. But yes. I'm needed here."

"So, you'll come back?"

"I will. When the violence allows us to re-insert. They want me back in Paris until then."

"Let's stay in touch, Sven. If you ever get out to San Diego, stop by. I'd like to hear about your travels."

They shared contact information.

"Thanks again," said Sven as he started to leave.

Tucker had an unanswered question. "Why did they remove the doctor's hand?"

"One of them had been badly injured. They originally came to us for medical treatment. We couldn't refuse, of course, but the man was near death. Lisle did everything she could. We had to amputate the man's leg, and he still died. It was her punishment. They were crazy with hatred for her. When they came to take the body home, I thought they'd kill us all."

"That's tough."

"You survive. We just stuck together to survive. I had her pretty well drugged up when they did it. Nothing I could do because they threatened the other women. We tried to fix her up, but without proper supplies, I feared for the worse."

"The American girl. She tough enough to deal with all this?" asked Tucker.

"You want the truth? She was a spoiled brat. Should I feel bad for saying so?"

"No, I understand."

"Her first trip. It's not fair."

"What were their intentions?"

"They were looking to hook up with a larger militia. The girl was for their General. I think they'd have executed us when they met up, but that's just a guess."

Kyle arrived. "How's he doing?"

"I gave him some Ativan. He'll get a good sleep."

"Okay, good." He turned to Sven. "When do you take off?"

"Waiting to hear, but soon. I fly back to Paris."

"Gotcha. Thanks for your assistance. Jean told me about your background. Sure you don't want to come join us? We could always use a good man," Kyle said.

"It's a long story. I told Tucker here. We'll stay in touch." Sven shook Kyle's hand, waved to Tucker, and was gone.

"How're you doing?"

"I'm hanging. I snuck a call to Brandy after we got here. Hope you don't mind."

"Nah, that's good. Get some rest. Just stay with Brawley. I'll bring by some food later so hopefully you can get a couple hours of sleep, okay?"

"Thanks. What about you?"

Kyle leaned over and looked at Brawley again. "I'll get my sleep on the plane. I promised I'd call Dorie, so probably do that now."

"Right."

"Welcome back, Tucker. You did good."

"Then why am I not celebrating?"

"Because we lost one. Remind me next time not to plan a mission a week before the country is going to erupt into civil war, okay?"

"It's the first thing I'll ask, Kyle."

"You think he'll sort out?"

It hurt inside to lie to Kyle. "I think so. But he's going to need more time."

"And maybe he's done," said Kyle.

"He's only got two and a half more years to his twenty. Would be a shame."

Kyle nodded. He placed a hand on Tucker's shoulder. "Get some rest."

CHAPTER 19

THE NEXT DAY, Brandy got the text that they were about to depart Africa. It would take nearly twenty-four hours for him to get home. She was filled with relief and a growing anticipation. She knew that Tucker had done his job. Now it was time for her real job to begin.

Brandy was relieved that Dorie's frank call with Kyle had helped her deal with the future she was going to face. She contacted Dr. Brownlee and asked his help again to have Brawley admitted to the same clinic he'd been at before. Dr. Brownlee took time to walk her through what would be going on this time and generously offered to underwrite whatever the VA wouldn't cover with the hospitalization, as his family had done before.

She'd spent the day yesterday with Dorie and Jessica, but now was home, preparing for Tucker's return. She'd spoken with several of the wives on her phone list and offered to babysit or run errands. Everyone was in the same boat: waiting for their men to come back. She got many pieces of advice, some of it not helpful, but she felt mentally strong and ready.

THE AIRFIELD AT Coronado was windy as Brandy lined up with the other wives, waiting for the transport to arrive. Kids were decked out in their finest, some of them pulled from school so they could welcome their daddies home. Following tradition, the families occupied a small hangar away from the rest of the public, and the kids, who had grown up with each other since infants, had completely taken over the facility.

Dorie smiled to her as she waited with two attendants, who would be assisting Brawley to the clinic. Jessica sat close to her mother and was playing with items she found in her diaper bag.

As she scanned the little gathering, Brandy did feel part of this very large, growing family. It was the part of being with Tucker she hadn't expected. She had never felt alone during the short deployment and didn't feel alone now.

At last, the plane arrived. A hush fell over the room. Within minutes, men began to deplane. Kids were pointing, wives were crying and holding onto each other, and others were chasing their kids around the hangar. The men stood to attention, forming two lines as Ollie's flag-draped casket was lowered from the cargo bay, and several of the men carried it to the black waiting hearse. Ollie's mother was helped out of the hearse and then shook hands and hugged the men who had been with her son. She gave a long endearing hug to Brawley and spoke to him briefly. Brandy watched Brawley's arm slowly draw up to the woman's back to return part of the hug.

As the vehicle pulled away, Tucker looked strong, his jaw firm with resolve. He had an arm around Brawley, who walked clumsily as if his shoes were made of concrete. Tucker had both duty bags over his shoulder until Armando relieved him and remained in step. Brawley was working hard to keep up with the group. Many of the other men ran for the hangars as the families spilled out onto the tarmac in celebration.

She waited for him to be free before she saw him look for her. That's when she ran into his arms, colliding so hard they nearly toppled.

"There she is," he whispered in her ear. "I couldn't wait to get that body slam."

She drew back to search his face. He was back. He was totally back.

"Are you making a comment about my weight again?" she teased.

"Hell yes. I've always told you. You're perfect the way you are."

"So glad you're home, sweetheart." She was going to say more, but Tucker had covered her mouth. She tried to mumble through.

"Shut up, Brandy. Let me kiss you proper."

HAVING TUCKER HOME was like starting out all over again. She found herself shy undressing around him until the familiarity returned. She was surprised it had changed so in the brief time since he'd been gone. But their routine returned. They talked at night and slept in late.

She'd been prepared for a lack of enthusiasm for sex, which was part of the advice some of her friends had given her. Tucker was the opposite. He was obsessed with her, driven to follow her around with a perpetual hard-on. She wondered if it would start being annoying after a while, he was so much under foot. If they bumped into each other in the kitchen, it turned into sex. She got partially dressed, only to have it turn into sex. She found herself wondering if she was keeping up with him, his need had grown so.

He read her his journal in little excerpts but kept it privately tucked away. Brandy was overjoyed he planned to continue writing, though. His entries made her feel like she was right there with him.

"You could be a writer, Tucker. Your writing is very clear. You paint such vivid pictures. I'm so happy you've learned to enjoy it."

"Didn't know I liked to write. Now that I've found my voice, I'm going to explore it further. It's like second nature, something that I find easy to do. Who knew this big guy could do it? Gives me something to think about when the time comes after I'm off the Teams."

"Oh, you could write thrillers!"

"Sexy thrillers," he whispered.

Even the discussion about writing led to sex.

AFTER A WEEK, she started going back to her father's store, giving Tucker some alone time. He also wanted to schedule a visit with Brawley. It would take a few days to arrange.

As if the knowledge of this visit coming up added a burden, the happy veneer of his homecoming began to fade slowly in the weeks that followed. He became less interested in her work at the store or in helping her dad with the garden. Their sexual encounters became less frequent as well. He'd spent time with Kyle and others, and she could see he was worried the Navy was considering medically discharging Brawley. Tucker wanted to defend his best friend with a burning desire she'd not seen in him before.

He'd had discussions about their mission and she learned from Dorie that the Navy had been unhappy with the Team's performance. Not only had they lost a man, but the Navy questioned Kyle's judgment about bringing Brawley on the mission, as well as the mission itself. There was a chance Kyle himself had lost favor with his superiors. She knew Tucker took it hard, like he was partially responsible for it.

She felt the Brotherhood was pulling Tucker away from her.

As the days drew closer to his first visit with Brawley, Tucker's demeanor became more reserved.

Little arguments cropped up. She became worried, and asked if everything was okay with his position on the Teams. Tucker reared up and spat back a question.

"Where the hell did you get that? You think there's something wrong with me? That I didn't do my job well?"

"No, Tucker. I'm just trying to help. In case you want to talk."

"About what? There are some things I have to keep to myself. Quit trying so hard, Brandy. It pisses me off."

It was impossible to even talk about little things without her comments causing offense. Finally, on the morning he was to visit the clinic, the two of them had a major fight.

"Quit asking if I'm okay. You act like you're afraid of me, afraid of what I've done. You're walking around on egg shells, Brandy, asking too many dumb questions. Do I do anything that makes you think I'm not okay?" Tucker shouted at her.

"You're misunderstanding me, Tucker. What I'm asking is what's going on with you? Because I see a change. That's all. I see a hardness in you I didn't see before."

Tucker's body reacted. His fists balled, and he held his jaw clamped down tight, without a glimmer of anything soft. She knew she wasn't going to like what he had to say next.

"I'm not going to even dignify that comment with a response. Does everything have to be happy, happy, happy all the time? Why do I have to keep reassuring you? This isn't about you. It's about standing for my teammate, defending him, because right now, he can't do it himself. I won't leave him behind, and if you can't understand that, then you never really knew me, Brandy."

His hard stare scared her. She was on shaky ground and didn't want to escalate the tension between them, but she was confused, worried why he was reacting so personally.

Tears collected and began to stream down her face.

"Don't do that!" He barked. "That's not fair. You've got to stop hovering around me like some butterfly and just let me handle my own shit."

She knew he felt bad for her. But she could also see he wasn't going to back down.

"Brandy," he said as he softened his voice, "there are some things about me that you can't be a part of. There are things you have to just trust me on. Stop prying. Stop needing to know everything about every thought and emotion I have. I don't like or want that."

She remembered the conversations they'd had when they first met, about how he'd never let anyone into his life before. Had that all changed now? And why so quickly?

Brandy's insides melted. She felt the barrier between them, that a line had been crossed, and knew that he didn't trust her with some of his secrets. It would be a mistake to try to reason, convince, or otherwise try to manipulate him, but she was deeply hurt.

The best thing she could do was not make it worse. It didn't feel right, but she stuffed down her emotions, took a deep breath, and found some backbone. She wiped the tears from her cheeks.

"Well, you let me know when the other Tucker comes home. I'll be waiting. You go ahead and be the way you have to be. I'm not going to apologize for my tears or try to change the way you're feeling. It's like what you told Brawley. I can only go so far. You have to meet me halfway, Tucker."

She watched his truck pull out of the driveway on his way to see Brawley. She hoped that the man she loved would be the one coming back after the visit. He hadn't said good-bye or given her a kiss. He didn't notice she was standing there, her heart worried—not broken, but drained.

This sudden change between them was harder than the concern she had when he was deployed.

Should I feel this way? What is happening?

CHAPTER 20

T UCKER CRANKED THE music up in his truck and tried to set aside their argument. He didn't want to figure out what he was feeling. Best to just push it out of his mind. He needed a blank slate when he talked to Brawley. He needed to be ready for anything he observed with his friend. Today wasn't the day to analyze the argument with his wife.

The clinic was bright and clean, not like some re-hab facilities he'd been to in past years run by the VA.

He asked for Brawley at reception. The young attendant batted her eyes at him, making an obvious flirtation, and it pissed him off. She'd pushed a clip-board across the counter at him.

"Why do I have to fill this out?" He'd worked not to use any smacktalk or swearwords.

"Well," she said in her pert little way, "we keep track of all our visitors. As I'm sure you're aware, this is a mental health clinic, and, well, we're very protective of our clients."

Tucker thought it laughable she regarded Brawley as a client. He nearly threw the clipboard at her.

"But I *have* an appointment! It took like two weeks to get that appointment. You have to examine me as well before I can go in there?" He pointed with his thumb down the hall. Several people in the waiting room stopped their conversation and looked up.

An older, matronly woman appeared behind the young receptionist. She angled her head closer, noting his SEAL Team 3 shirt, speaking in a low tone so the audience around them wouldn't be further alerted. "Don't take it out on her, sir. She's just doing her job." The woman gave him a spiteful sneer, whispering through her teeth. "And I don't care who the hell you think you are. Even as a Navy SEAL, you won't get to see him until you fill out the paperwork. Navy's rules, sir, not mine."

She stood back a step, straightened her form, and plastered a smile on her face. Tucker never had hit a woman, but he wanted to hit this one. He knew it wouldn't be smart, and he did his practiced deep breathing technique until his ire dissipated. Clutching the clipboard, he took it over to an armed chair and prepared the form. He nearly shattered the pencil gripped in his hand.

As he was signing the bottom, a young woman appeared in front of him, wearing a white lab coat.

"I'm Dr. Christen Saunders. You must be Tucker Hudson?" She held out her hand.

The doctor had a firm handshake, her bright blue eyes peering deep into his. Her attractiveness was probably her secret weapon as Tucker found it hard to stay angry standing before her.

"Yes, I'm here to see Brawley Hanks," he mumbled as he stood.

"Can I have that?" She pointed to the clipboard. Tucker gave it up.

"We've been expecting you, Tucker. May I call you Tucker, or would you prefer another term to address you?"

"Tucker's fine," he answered. He shifted his weight and felt exposed, speaking to the doctor in front of so many prying eyes.

"If you could follow me?"

He walked beside her, looking over his shoulder at the large woman behind the desk who was still protecting her turf and her protégé.

"Carmen can be a little harsh at times, but we've recently had some issues with some of our patient's rights being violated. I understand Brawley has been here before. These are new procedures."

"No problem."

As they continued down a highly polished wide

hallway decorated with paintings done by patients and some by staff, he asked her how Brawley was doing.

"He's moving forward." She stopped. "Most guys like Brawley will be fine outside on their own, and can live normal, effective lives, eventually. But he's going to always react to stress in ways perhaps you or I wouldn't react. And I want to warn you, I doubt you'll be able to take him on future missions. I tell you this," she lowered her voice as a patient slipped by in a wheelchair, "because he's spent a lot of time talking about you two. He's very concerned how you think of him."

"Understood. Thank you, doctor."

They began walking again. "So my admonition is to make this a very light meeting. Don't stay too long, but come back soon. Tell him things he'll like hearing. Just reconnect. It will do him a world of good."

Tucker recalled his argument with Brandy this morning, especially the "happy, happy, happy" comment, and it annoyed him. "You want me to lie to him?"

"No. Just steer the conversation so you don't have to, and keep it to things he likes."

Tucker stopped this time. "But he likes the adventure of being on the Teams. He lives for that."

"Then you'll have to find something else he likes just as well. Just as intensely." Her pretty eyelids fluttered, and in his single days, he'd have found her attractive because she had an edge to her he liked. This gave him an idea.

"Do you get along with him?" Tucker asked.

"Oh yes. I think we have a very frank relationship. He's really coming along well. I've seen his chart from before, and he doesn't have any of the memory losses."

"Okay, good. Thank you, doctor."

When they arrived at Brawley's open door, Dr. Saunders greeted him cheerily. "We have a surprise for you today, Brawley."

"Oh yea?" Brawley smiled back at her and then looked to the side and made eye contact with Tucker.

"Fuckin' A! It took you long enough!" Brawley crossed the room in one leap and grabbed Tucker in a big bear hug.

Dr. Saunders turned and headed for the doorway. "Hey, you don't have to go. We could have a three-some," yelled Brawley.

Tucker saw the pretty doctor blush, examining the two of them. "Back in the day, you two would have been exactly the kinds of bad boys I'd have been delighted to sit with. But that was then. This is now. This is about you getting well and going home, Brawley." She looked down briefly and then whispered, wrinkling her nose, "But thanks."

She left the room.

Tucker knew his brief discussion with Brawley was

going to be all about the doctor.

TUCKER AGREED TO meet Brawley again in a few days and asked him to get the doctor to expedite his appointment so he didn't have to wait so long. Brawley was in near tears at the prospect Tucker had to leave.

"I don't want to do anything to jeopardize your stay and treatment here. We want you out."

"But we didn't get to talk about the guys. What happened to everyone? I barely remember it."

"Next time. Promise," Tucker said as he left.

He reported in to Kyle who told him a few of the guys were getting together for beers at the Scupper. Tucker was all in for that one.

The two boat crew guys were there, which was a surprise. He hadn't seen them since he got back. "Amigos!" he shouted as they greeted him. Several others sat at their favorite table next to the fire pit.

"Kinda feels like old times, right?" said T.J. Talbot. "Nice fire, stars out tonight." He broke into a grin.

Several of the team clinked long-necked beer bottles, and Tucker shivered. "Not anxious to do another one of those campouts."

"I agree. The rangers are fuckin' mean," quipped Fredo. "I'd have to say downright nasty."

Kyle asked him about his visit with Brawley.

"Well, hey, not sure if this is the case, but I'd say

he's getting better because of his doctor. Kyle, have you been by yet?"

"Nope. Wanted to see how it went with you first. But she briefed me by phone."

"Well, I don't know if her phone voice is sexy, but man, she's a looker. Very nice too. A little tough, but fun." He winked and the guys cheered.

"Now, don't get ideas, Tucker," said Cooper. "Old married man means just that, my friend."

"Hey. I was doing it for Brawley!" said Tucker.

One by one, he made eye contact with the team and one by one, he saw in their faces that in his first mission, he'd passed with flying colors.

"You knock up that pretty wife of yours yet, Tucker? Now would be a good time," teased Jameson.

"Some are working on it harder than others, I hear, Jameson," added DeWayne Huggles. "He's got the finger piano action going on!"

Again, a chorus of cheers let out. Someone poured a beer on the Nashville SEAL.

But the comment had struck a nerve with Tucker and he'd lost his lightheartedness. He'd left Brandy in a state he wasn't proud of. He'd have to watch that, he noted.

It felt good to be with the guys, in the warm night in San Diego, and it even felt good to get a bit of a buzz on. Tucker knew he'd have to order something or he'd have to take a cab home. The waitress was overloaded, and the wait would be extensive. So, while everyone was jabbering on about being back home, Tucker slipped into the bar to order a burger.

"We can bring it out to you," the bartender told him.

"Thanks."

Tucker was on his way back to the table with four new brews when he nearly ran into Shayla, his ex. Her eyes widened as she hungrily devoured the sight of him in front of her.

"Well, look who got out of the cage tonight. My favorite sailor." She glanced over to her bevy of friends sitting in a dark corner.

Tucker wasn't having any of it. "Not in the mood."

"If you change your mind, call me." She put her hands on his chest, sliding them down his jacket, yanking and tugging on his pockets. Tucker nudged her away.

"Shayla, why do you do this? It's totally beneath you. I have absolutely no interest in having anything to do with you ever again, so do me a favor and butt out of my life."

"Well, sailor, didn't mean to get you all hot and bothered." She leaned into him and whispered, "You do remember those days, don't you?"

"I honestly don't," Tucker said and walked outside.

An hour later, the group had pared down to just Tucker, Kyle, Cooper and T.J. As he hoped, the burger had helped take the edge off.

"You hear anything from Sven?" Kyle asked him.

"Not yet. I will. I think you will too," Tucker answered. "You hear from Jean?"

Kyle frowned. "Yea. The guy's whole world has fallen apart. They seized all his property, and he barely got out with his life before the militia came through. Some of his men defected."

"That surprises me," said Coop.

"They had families they had to protect. It's the story of Africa, Middle East too. They'll fight for whomever will protect their family."

Everyone agreed.

"So he's back in France?" asked T.J.

"He is. For now. He's still looking into what happened with the American nurse. But he doesn't have much hope, and there's not much he can do from Paris."

The conversation got sober in a hurry. "Crying shame," whispered Tucker.

"You think they'd ever send us back in to get her?" Coop asked.

"Maybe another team. Not sure I'll get that chance," Kyle said with resignation. "Although this *is* our deployment window. Depends on when they find her. Jean told me not to hold my breath."

Tucker didn't want to ask if Kyle was considering leaving the Teams or if he felt his career in the Navy was on hold. He wanted to have that private conversation with him about Brawley without other ears. He asked about the Belgium doctor.

"Understand she fully recovered, and has a prosthetic hand, Jean says. He was encouraging her to get a hook!"

"Serve anyone right if they tried to mess with her," said Tucker.

Everyone laughed.

Tucker knew it was time to leave. Before he was tempted with another beer, excused himself and said his good-byes. "I like this. Let's do it again, sooner," he suggested.

"We were just talking about that when you arrived," answered Cooper.

THE DRIVE HOME felt longer than the trip over. The house was dark, but Brandy had left the porch light on. He removed his jacket, tossing it on the chair, and kicked off his shoes. He sat on the couch and stared at the blank TV screen.

Normally, Brandy would have greeted him just as soon as he came through the door. But after their argument today, he figured he deserved what he got. So he sat in the dark and just thought about things. He thought about taking a shot of Jack, but lost interest.

So much was out of his control. He thought about the poor American nurse, about the misfortune Jean had gone through. Brawley, he wasn't worried about any longer, or at least not for now. Getting the Navy to keep him in might be something Kyle could help him with. The guys were good. He knew Sven was probably enjoying Paris.

But that left Brandy. She was the glue that made everything hold together. He realized that loud and clear when he saw Shayla at the Scupper. The differences between these two women were like the two sides of the moon. He remembered what Kyle had told him at the bonfire before they left, *'You got a good one there, Tucker.'*

It was true.

But it also wasn't fair to her if he couldn't get as close to her as she needed. He'd been fine with long distance friendships and casual hookups. But Brandy wanted everything, wanted it intense. Believed in the happily ever after. She wanted every part of him, and he wasn't sure he could give it. Sometimes, he was all on. Sometimes he was just switched off. And it could happen quickly too. Maybe he'd been lying to himself. He never wanted to lie to her. She deserved so much more.

He knew it was time to go back and apologize. Maybe that would help him remove all the rough skin and the worry. Nothing was ever one hundred percent perfect, especially a homecoming.

Just like no mission was.

He opened the door to the bedroom a crack just to watch her sleep. Moonlight showered her arm and shoulder with silver. Her hair splayed all over the pillow. He vowed he'd try harder. If he couldn't get to where she wanted him to be, like she said, she could go only halfway. If he couldn't go the rest of it, well, he'd go as far as he could, out of honor for how hard she was working. How devoted she was.

He sat on the bed and removed his pants, trying not to make noise. He took off his SEAL Team 3 shirt and slipped into the sheets with just his stars and stripes boxers on. The warm mattress melted the kinks in his shoulder and thighs. He crept closer until he could spoon behind her, trying not to wake her up.

Her smell filled his nose as he lay his head down in the nest of her hair, his lips so close to her neck he could kiss her. And then his hand was on her hip as she slowly moved, pressing her backside into him and letting him feel the length of her body. His hand slipped down her thigh. She turned to her back, drawing up her nightgown so his fingers could feel her flesh. Her smooth inner thigh was magic to touch. She inhaled, arched back, covered his fingers with her hand and drew him up to her core.

She dropped her hand while he felt her wet heat, slipping through the petals of her labia. She moaned, and he lost all his control. He climbed on top, pulling her to him with one arm under her waist. Her beautiful breasts called to him in the moonlight. He didn't take the time to remove his boxers, or her gown, but found himself inside her, thrusting deep, and desperate to be deeper.

She writhed beneath him, already feeling an orgasm blooming and sending rivulets of passion down where their thighs slid against each others'. She reached between them and felt their joining, tears streaming down her cheeks, dropping like diamonds into the pillow.

He was going to spill, and he felt awful it was so quick. That's not the way he'd wanted it to be.

"Brandy," he started to whisper.

She covered his mouth with her fingers. "Shhhh."

"But Brandy—"

She stopped him again. As he started to come inside her, she held his face between her hands and whispered, "It's all perfect, Tucker."

CHAPTER 21

WHILE LAST NIGHT'S lovemaking was a gift, Brandy also knew that it didn't necessarily mean everything was back to normal. But it did encourage her that he sought her engagement, that he came to her, instead of the other way around.

She made coffee, leaving Tucker to sleep in as long as he wanted to. She sat on the sofa with her knees pulled to her chin. She stretched her nightgown over her legs, grasped the coffee mug to her chest and sipped the warm mixture.

She knew some of her friends would disapprove of her actions last night—just jumping right back in bed with him without getting things aired out first. Maybe that worked for most marriages. Maybe it was the healthiest way. But that might also be the way she'd lose him. She knew men of action were different and that she'd actually married two men, not one. Now that he had gotten re-acquainted with his other self, she'd

have to accept the other side of him if she wanted their
marriage to work.

Brandy always wanted to understand the why of it
all, to feel things, figure out situations and people.
Tucker was different. He was act now and think about
the consequences later. Maybe he never doubted
himself like she did. Or, maybe he just did a better job
of either covering it up or charging ahead anyway.

Tucker cracked open the bedroom door and padded out to the kitchen for his coffee. His stars and
stripes boxers were bunched up in his butt crack, but
he was still a delicious package with his enormous
shoulders, muscled back, and bundled thighs. He had
more scars on him than she'd noticed before. He
turned, his body facing her, but continued to look
down at his coffee. She glanced away and waited for
him to say something.

"I want to apologize, Brandy."

That got her attention.

He took another sip and collapsed his enormous
frame in the nearby arm chair, dwarfing it. She could
tell he was thinking, choosing his words carefully. She
decided to test his capacity for a little humor.

"Well, to be honest, I didn't think the sex last night
was all that bad."

Tucker's head whipped around, his expression one
of shock.

She continued, "don't apologize on my behalf. I had a good time." She tried to keep a very straight face as she peered at him over her mug.

His grin was slow to develop, but when he finished, she enjoyed just looking at him sitting there with his knees spread, nearly bare, the enormous tent in his pants extremely prominent. Suddenly, she was dripping with desire.

"I can do better."

She sipped her coffee quietly and ignored him, again working hard not to smile.

"Did you hear me?" he repeated.

"I'm ignoring you," she said. She knew she had piqued his interest big time.

"Okay, so I deserve this. I'm sorry, Brandy, for the argument yesterday morning."

It was a good start. "I'll try not to ask so many questions. But will you do something for me?"

"Within reason," he said as he finished off his coffee and set it on the coffee table.

"If you want to be left alone, just tell me. Don't snap at me. Give me a heads-up, and I'll learn to deal with it." Her eyes teared up, but she fought to make sure they didn't overflow. "Don't push me out like that, and I promise to put away my butterfly wings."

"Come here, Brandy," he said softly.

She knew that he wanted sex, but as she sat in his

lap and curled herself against his chest, she felt his careful, protective arms surrounded her. There were no strings. They sat together in the early morning space that was their life.

It wasn't perfect, but it was what they had. And that was indeed quite enough.

THAT EVENING, BRANDY and Tucker went out to dinner with her father and his new girlfriend, Jillian.

"I've heard so much about you," Jillian said as they were seated. "What you do is incredible, Tucker. I have nothing but respect."

Tucker was polite but dodged questions about what their last mission had been, except to say they were in Africa and there had been a hostage rescue operation. He stopped short of calling the mission successful.

Steven Cook held Jillian's hand. "We've got some news to share with you."

Brandy held her breath, having a good idea what it was about.

"Jillian's agreed to marry me, Brandy." He smiled as Jillian snuggled closer. "We'd like your—" He backed up to correct himself. "We'd like both of your blessings. It's important to us."

"Oh, Dad. I'm so happy." Brandy stood, and danced over to hug her dad first, and then Jillian.

Tucker put his hand over theirs and said, "Way to

go, guys. I think that's a wonderful idea. Brandy and I are both on board."

"And there's more," her dad began. "We've been giving a lot of thought to the store. And I think I want to sell it," he added. "The way things stand, we're awfully tied down. We could do more travel, and you know, Brandy, that's what I've wanted to do for years."

"Can you find a buyer?" Tucker asked.

"We think we have one," said Jillian. "There's a family from Mexico, second generation Americans, and they'd like to convert the store to something that caters to the Latino population. They can carry special-ty foods, keep some of the deli items and the fruit, but add other ethnic things. They own two catering trucks already. It would be perfect for them."

Brandy was delighted. "Sounds like the perfect plan."

"One more thing. Jillian has the house by the ocean," her dad began. "So why don't you two move into the big house? I'd like to deed half of it, your mother's half, to you, Brandy, before we get married. It's something she'd want me to do. You can do whatever you want with it. Sell it, refinance it and pay off my half, buy something else—anything you want."

"Dad, I don't know what to say." Brandy was over-whelmed with her father's generosity. It was nothing she'd ever imagined would happen.

Steve Cook laughed. "I know it's a lot to consider, so you guys think about it. You don't have to let us know tonight. You might want to go get something of your own. In that case, I'll sell the property and give you half."

ON THE WAY home, Tucker asked her if she had any thoughts about her father's proposal.

She watched his strong profile, lights from the highway splashing colors inside the cab of the truck. "What do you think?"

"I think it's your decision." He kissed her hand. His eyes briefly connected with hers. "Okay?"

She thought perhaps she'd need more time, but all of a sudden, it became clear. Because of her dad's generosity, they were living in the bungalow behind the big house that her parents had lived in. That big house would always be her parent's house long after they were both gone.

Tucker arrived home and sat in the driveway, turning off the engine. He put his arm around her and let her think.

"Tucker, this property was chosen and belonged to my parents. They've moved on with their lives." She looked up to his face. "I think I'd like to move on with ours. I'd like to find *our* house. Together."

"So be it," he said, just before he kissed her.

IN THE WEEKS following, the store ownership papers were drawn up. Brandy's father put the property on the market and it sold in one week for way more than they'd ever thought possible. During the escrow, Brandy and Tucker packed up their household, put some of their belongings in storage, and temporarily moved into a rental near Brawley and Dorie's home until they could find their perfect place.

Tucker also spent time with Brawley, who improved so quickly he was released from the clinic. Dorie's pregnancy was progressing, and Brawley was looking forward to the new little one.

But still unresolved was Brawley's future on the Teams. Everyone held their breath and waited.

CHAPTER 22

T UCKER WAS AT the Scupper with several of the
  other teammates when he got a call from Brawley.

"They tossed me," Brawley said.

"No way."

"Yup. Got the letter when we got home tonight. I'm
to get a medical discharge."

"But your pension. You get that?"

"Yes, but I'm a secretary or some shit until I get my
twenty years in. I'm a desk jockey."

"No harm in that, Brawley."

The more he thought about it, the more relieved he
was. The Navy had taken away the possibility Brawley
could go out and get himself killed, or worse, get
someone else killed. He remembered what Dr. Saunders had told him.

This was actually good news.

"You could go become a BUD/S instructor, Brawley."

"I was thinking about that."

"Take all your frustrations out on those froglets. Would you have the heart to do that?"

"The way I look at it, if they'd have me, I'd be saving their lives. Those brothers would be solid, kick ass."

"Well then, let's work on it tomorrow. We'll get Collins on it. With Kyle's recommendation, I think you'd be a shoe-in."

Tucker didn't want to push, but he sensed there was something else Brawley wasn't telling him. "Dorie's got to be relieved, man."

"She's in shock. But yea, I think she's pretty cool with it. As long as I am. Tucker, I can't be pushing papers around."

"Why not? It's all support. You'd still be helping Teams operate. It's just that you wouldn't be stuck in the jungle, getting shot at, getting sick, or walking into a trap."

"I wanted to get those motherfuckers who took out Ollie."

"How many Team guys retire and feel like they've gotten all the bad guys?"

"Nobody does."

"Exactly, Brawley. And it wasn't your fault."

Again, there was a pause. Tucker got annoyed.

"You're not drinking, are you?"

"Nope. No more of that. I'm on my meds regular,

too."

"You tell your father yet?"

"Nope. I'm going to bring you along when we do that."

Tucker completely understood. "I'll be there for you." He kept listening for something more but finally gave up. "Well, if there isn't anything else, I gotta get home to the wife." He tried one more time. "Brawley, are you sure there isn't anything else?"

Tucker heard him exhale. "Well, we got another piece of news today as well."

"At last! I knew there was something. Spill it."

"We had a fun visit at the doctor's. Dorie and I are having twins."

A WEEK LATER, Tucker took Brawley to his interview with the Commander on base. Kyle stood up for Brawley, he said. They'd asked that he retain his SEAL rank, and do his last two years as a BUD/S instructor.

"I was surprised, because you know, he's a bit on their shit list."

"That's totally misplaced, in my opinion," Tucker said.

They were watching the BUD/S class running drills on the beach. The pickup with the DOR, Drop On Request, bell was slowly making its way in front of a crowd of about twenty young men, running in sand with their combat boots on. And it was a race. One of the instructors, who sat on the tailgate was yelling something with his bullhorn.

Tucker punched Brawley. "You gotta think that would be fun."

"Yea, well, we'll see what they say. I might be processing DORs too."

"Even that wouldn't be too hard. You did it. You made it and served, stuck out eighteen years."

"Don't remind me. That's two short of my dad."

"I'm sure he doesn't care about that. He wants you alive, and whole."

"He does. We had a good talk."

"Excellent. So what do they think about the twins?"

"Biggest smile I've seen my mom sport in about three years. She was almost giddy, Tucker."

"No shit?"

"Honest. Even my old man mentioned it. Said she looked ten years younger."

"Holy smoke. Happy for you, Brawley."

"How about you guys. Still looking for a house?"

"Yup. Brandy has been busy with all that. Christy has been helping her look. Soon. I think it will be very soon now."

"Don't you have a say?" Brawley asked.

"Are you fuckin' kidding me? I had one friend who picked out the house for their family when they moved east, and they fuckin' got a divorce. I'm not that stupid, Brawley. A house is a house. I've lived in a bunch of them. If she's happy, then I'm happy."

"Tucker, you're a smart man."

He chuckled. "It's because of all the mistakes I've made."

They spent the rest of the evening over at the Scupper, meeting several of the Team. It was still Tucker's job to keep Brawley connected, and that was the best way to do it. He had to cut out early, because Brandy said she was trying out something new, some kind of special dinner.

Tucker was looking forward to it.

CHAPTER 23

BRANDY HAD PREPARED this special evening in her mind for months. She'd had several close calls, but at last, she confirmed with the doctor that she was pregnant. She'd been worried, since she was certain she'd been pregnant a couple of other times but wound up with a late period, dashing her hopes. He estimated she was nearly four months along. She had no symptoms whatsoever, except for her expanding chest.

The two of them hadn't discussed the timing of having a child, but they weren't using protection, either. Now they'd have to start looking in earnest for a new home. She was tired of living in the tiny studio, looking for things in boxes nearly every day.

She bought Tucker's favorite red wine and a ribeye from the specialty meat market that had just opened up on the island. She was making his favorite garlic mashed potatoes. She hoped he'd still be hungry and made him promise to be home early.

The table was set. She lit candles around the kitchen and living room, plus one in the bedroom. The salad mix was chilling, and the wine had been opened. Tucker was fussy about his meat, so that part would fall to him, but the lean steak was peppered just the way he liked it, waiting on the grill.

She had just a few things to finish before he was due home. She picked up a load from the laundry and sat on the bed, folding. She hung up two of his shirts and discovered a jacket he'd misplaced during their move had fallen on the floor of the closet and somehow had gotten shoved to the back corner.

She shook it out, gave it a smell, and decided it didn't pass the test. There was no question the last time he'd worn it was at the Scupper. There was only one place that had that aroma in all of San Diego County.

She checked his pockets because Tucker was forgetful, often leaving cough drops or pieces of gum which made a mess in the dryer. In his front pocket was a slip of paper, which she removed.

She thought perhaps her eyes were deceiving her. Her body began to shake, and so she sat down on the bed. Between her fingers, someone had written in blue pen the name Shayla and included a phone number. It wasn't Tucker's handwriting.

Brandy felt she might become sick, so she put her head between her knees and took several deep breaths.

How did I miss this? Is that where he's been going lately? How could I have been so blind?

This wasn't going to be the happy evening she'd planned. Could Shayla have come into their life during those weeks when he was so aloof? Did this woman swoop in and steal her husband back from her at his most vulnerable time?

Or, and this was worse, was Tucker pretending to be the loyal husband, while he fooled around and played the field. Except he'd made a mistake. A grave mistake.

There was a tiny voice in the back of her head trying to tell her something, but she hit it with a baseball bat. Except for her heartbeat pounding in her ears, the chatter was gone.

Think! Think! Should I pack? Should I lock the door and make him go away? Or should I listen to his explanation, even if it was a lie?

She heard Tucker's truck pull up. She checked her face then brought the jacket into the living room, to wait for him to walk through the door. She left all the lights out and the candles on as she heard his footsteps, and, at last, the door handle turning.

"Whoa! This is nice," he said, turning around to find her. He dropped his keys by the door and removed his shoes. "Something smells heavenly with lots of garlic." He paused and then called out again, "Brandy?

Are you here?"

"I'm here, Tucker," she said.

"What's up, sweetheart?"

He came over to her and bent down. She turned away.

"Hey, what's up?" he said as he sat beside her. "You found my jacket, I see."

When she looked at him, he suddenly recognized what kind of an emotional state she was in. Brandy wondered if he knew yet that he'd been caught. His forehead wrinkled as he frowned.

"You're upset. Tell me." He reached for her hand, and she withdrew it.

"I found your jacket. Inside one of your pockets, I found this." She held the slip of paper up in front of his eyes.

"May I?" he asked politely.

She gave him Shayla's note. His eyes were angry as he stared at the note and then searched her face. "You don't think—?"

"I don't know what to think, Tucker. How about you explain this to me?"

"I've never seen it in my life."

"It was in your *jacket*. Why would you have her phone number, and I'm thinking she wrote it there for you. Isn't that her handwriting—?"

"I have no idea. Honest, Brandy, I've never seen it.

You certainly don't think I've been seeing her? Is that what you think?"

"Give me a better explanation, Tucker. I'm all ears."

"I can't stand the bitch. I don't know how—" He stopped, leaned back into the sofa, and hit his forehead with his palm. "My first night out at the Scupper after we got back, she was there with her little witches' harem. I bumped into her in the bar."

"You were flirting with her."

"I was trying to get out of her way. I had four beers I was trying to take out to the table. She practically slammed into me and—" He stopped again. "She reached out, but I pushed her away. She must have slipped this into my pocket. I never saw it, Brandy. Honest. Since we've been together, I've never called her. I don't want to ever see her again."

Brandy heard all the laughter of her childhood years, when the kids at school teased her for being larger than the rest of the girls. She remembered the bridesmaids and how they gossiped at the wedding, how they treated her at the gym. Her defenses were strong, her reaction hard to the suspicion that perhaps she couldn't trust Tucker, that perhaps he too was a part of that crowd.

Her perfect life had gone up in smoke. She wasn't even hearing what Tucker was telling her, until she felt his hands on her arms as he turned her to look at him. He was asking her to look into his eyes.

"I swear to you, Brandy. There has never been anyone else since we met. I've not even considered this."

She blinked, watching him in slow motion say words she couldn't understand.

"You've imagined something that never happened, Brandy. I would never do this to you. Please, honey, trust me."

At last she heard him. Her body began to thaw. His pained expression broke her heart.

No, I've broken my own heart.

"You've never called her once?"

"Not once. I didn't know this was in my jacket. I'd lost my jacket, remember?"

She nodded. Her lower lip began to pucker.

"Man, do you have an imagination." He pressed the hair from her forehead. "I love you, Brandy. I always will. But please, when you think something like this has happened—I don't care what it is. Just ask me. You wanted me to give you a heads-up when I wanted to be alone. Can I ask you to give me the benefit of the doubt?"

She nodded again. She was ashamed. She placed her palm against his cheek. "Tucker, I'm so sorry I doubted you. I made a fool of myself."

He held her to his chest. "No worries. I want you to

trust me completely. I'm going to work hard to make sure you know you can." He smiled and then kissed her. "But you do have a wicked imagination!" He followed up his comment with a chuckle.

"I wanted this to be a special night until I found this."

"I was thinking for a moment I'd married an ax murderer. It was very gothic, Brandy. The whole scene was very dangerous. All these candles, with you sitting there in the dark giving me daggers."

Brandy found a little humor in this.

"Geez, honey. You kind of gave me a scare."

"You want some wine?"

"I think I'll have something stronger. So what's the special occasion?"

Brandy had really messed up her planned evening. As Tucker ran to the kitchen to get a drink, Brandy came up behind him, wrapping her arms around his waist. He stopped, turning around to face her again.

"I've got a nice ribeye steak, green salad mix and garlic mashed potatoes."

"This is unbelievable. You did all this for me? Or was it the ritual you needed to kill me?"

She bowed her head, feeling shy.

"I'm pregnant, Tucker. I went to the doctor today and verified it. You're going to be a father."

"Holy crap."

"That's not exactly what I was expecting."

"Well, look at all this. Do you think I was expecting this?"

She gave him a couple of minutes to let it sink in. He poured two glasses of the opened wine, and when she declined, he drank both of them.

"You know that evening we met? I knew right then and there my life would never be the same. I was having a miserable time, wishing I'd not come, and then you waltzed right into my life." He gave her another hug.

"I won't do something like this again, Tucker. You can trust me on that."

"I don't believe you, Brandy. But whatever it is, I'm going to love the hell out of it."

THE EVENING WAS indeed perfect after all. There was so much to live for, so much to look forward to. They celebrated with the wine, the food, and the ice cream afterwards.

They were headed to their bedroom when Tucker's cell phone rang. He hesitated.

"Should I see who it is?" He winked.

"Up to you. Go ahead, I'll meet you in bed."

She removed her clothes and put on the lacy bright red nightgown she'd purchased. Leaving one candle on, she slipped into the lavender-scented sheets and thought about what their child would look like.

A little Tucker?

Tucker's voice silenced. He stood in the doorway with his cell phone still gripped in his hand.

"That was Kyle. They found the American nurse."

Did you enjoy SEALed Forever? Want more? You can preorder the 4th book in the Bone Frog Brotherhood, SEAL's Rescue, here. It's Sharon's latest book!

sharonhamiltonauthor.com/sealed-forever

Here's the blurb:

Navy SEAL Tucker Hudson has barely recovered from his last difficult deployment in Africa, a near-failed operation, when he learns the American hostage they were unable to free that last time, has been found. His team is tasked with going in a second time to complete what was left undone.

Brandy Hudson's world is changing every day as she devotes herself to their new pregnancy and the purchase of their new home.

But danger from the hostage rescue across the oceans comes home to affect Brandy and Tucker's family in a desperate plot uncovered in California. Will it be in time to save the happily ever after they both desire?

Or, if you are new to Sharon Hamilton's SEALs and

want to read the original SEAL Brotherhood Series, the books that started it all from the beginning, order your Ultimate SEAL Collection #1 for the first 4 books, and Ultimate SEAL Collection #2 for the second three full length novels.

Want more SEALs? Check out her other SEALs series:

Band of Bachelors

Bad Boys of SEAL Team 3

Silver SEALs (multi-author collaborative)

Sleeper SEALs (multi-author collaborative)

Be sure to sign up for Sharon's Newsletter, follow her on Amazon or BookBub so you don't miss a thing!

ABOUT THE AUTHOR

NYT and USA/Today Bestselling Author Sharon Hamilton's SEAL Brotherhood series have earned her author rankings of #1 in Romantic Suspense, Military Romance and Contemporary Romance. Her other *Brotherhood* stand-alone series are: Bad Boys of SEAL Team 3, Band of Bachelors, True Blue SEALs, Nashville SEALs, Bone Frog Brotherhood, Sunset SEALs, Bone Frog Bachelor Series and SEAL Brotherhood Legacy Series. She is a contributing author to the very popular Shadow SEALs multi-author series.

Her SEALs and former SEALs have invested in two wineries, a lavender farm and a brewery in Sonoma County, which have become part of the new stories. They also have expanded to include Veteran-benefit projects on the Florida Gulf Coast, as well as projects in Africa and the Maldives. One of the SEAL wives has even launched her own women's fiction series. But old characters, as well as children of these SEAL heroes keep returning to all the newer books.

Sharon also writes sexy paranormals in two series: Golden Vampires of Tuscany and The Guardians.

A lifelong organic vegetable and flower gardener,

Sharon and her husband lived for fifty years in the Wine Country of Northern California, where many of her stories take place. Recently, they have moved to the beautiful Gulf Coast of Florida, with stories of shipwrecks, the white sugar-sand beaches of Sunset, Treasure Island and Indian Rocks Beaches.

She loves hearing from fans through her website: authorsharonhamilton.com

Find out more about Sharon, her upcoming releases, appearances and news when you sign up for Sharon's newsletter.

Facebook:
facebook.com/SharonHamiltonAuthor

Twitter:
twitter.com/sharonlhamilton

Pinterest:
pinterest.com/AuthorSharonH

Amazon:
amazon.com/Sharon-Hamilton/e/B004FQQMAC

BookBub:
bookbub.com/authors/sharon-hamilton

Youtube:
youtube.com/channel/UCDInkxXFpXp_4Vnq08ZxMBQ

Soundcloud:
soundcloud.com/sharon-hamilton-1

Sharon Hamilton's Rockin' Romance Readers:
facebook.com/groups/sealteamromance

Sharon Hamilton's Goodreads Group:
goodreads.com/group/show/199125-sharon-hamilton-readers-group

Visit Sharon's Online Store:
sharon-hamilton-author.myshopify.com

Join Sharon's Review Teams:

eBook Reviews:
sharonhamiltonassistant@gmail.com

Audio Reviews:
sharonhamiltonassistant@gmail.com

Life *is one fool thing after another.*
Love *is two fool things after each other.*

REVIEWS

PRAISE FOR THE
GOLDEN VAMPIRES OF TUSCANY SERIES

"Well to say the least I was thoroughly surprise. I have read many Vampire books, from Ann Rice to Kym Grosso and few other Authors, so yes I do like Vampires, not the super scary ones from the old days, but the new ones are far more interesting far more human then one can remember. I found Honeymoon Bite a totally engrossing book, I was not able to put it down, page after page I found delight, love, understanding, well that is until the bad bad Vamp started being really bad. But seeing someone love another person so much that they would do anything to protect them, well that had me going, then well there was more and for a while I thought it was the end of a beautiful love story that spanned not only time but, spanned Italy and California. Won't divulge how it ended, but I did shed a few tears after screaming but Sharon Hamilton did not let me down, she took me on amazing trip that I loved, look forward to reading another Vampire book of hers."

"An excellent paranormal romance that was exciting,

romantic, entertaining and very satisfying to read. It had me anticipating what would happen next many times over, so much so I could not put it down and even finished it up in a day. The vampires in this book were different from your average vampire, but I enjoy different variations and changes to the same old stuff. It made for a more unpredictable read and more adventurous to explore! Vampire lovers, any paranormal readers and even those who love the romance genre will enjoy Honeymoon Bite."

"This is the first non-Seal book of this author's I have read and I loved it. There is a cast-like hierarchy in this vampire community with humans at the very bottom and Golden vampires at the top. Lionel is a dark vampire who are servants of the Goldens. Phoebe is a Golden who has not decided if she will remain human or accept the turning to become a vampire. Either way she and Lionel can never be together since it is forbidden.

I enjoyed this story and I am looking forward to the next installment."

"A hauntingly romantic read. Old love lost and new love found. Family, heart, intrigue and vampires. Grabbed my attention and couldn't put down. Would definitely recommend."

PRAISE FOR THE
SEAL BROTHERHOOD SERIES

"Fans of Navy SEAL romance, I found a new author to feed your addiction. Finely written and loaded delicious with moments, Sharon Hamilton's storytelling satisfies like a thick bar of chocolate." —Marliss Melton, bestselling author of the *Team Twelve* Navy SEALs series

"Sharon Hamilton does an EXCELLENT job of fitting all the characters into a brotherhood of SEALS that may not be real but sure makes you feel that you have entered the circle and security of their world. The stories intertwine with each book before...and each book after and THAT is what makes Sharon Hamilton's SEAL Brotherhood Series so very interesting. You won't want to put down ANY of her books and they will keep you reading into the night when you should be sleeping. Start with this book...and you will not want to stop until you've read the whole series and then...you will be waiting for Sharon to write the next one." (5 Star Review)

"Kyle and Christy explode all over the pages in this first book, *[Accidental SEAL]*, in a whole new series of SEALs. If the twist and turns don't get your heart jumping, then maybe the suspense will. This is a must read for those that are looking for love and adventure with a little sloppy love thrown in for good measure." (5 Star Review)

PRAISE FOR THE
BAD BOYS OF SEAL TEAM 3 SERIES

"I love reading this series! Once you start these books, you can hardly put them down. The mix of romance and suspense keeps you turning the pages one right after another! Can't wait until the next book!" (5 Star Review)

"I love all of Sharon's Seal books, but *[SEAL's Code]* may just be her best to date. Danny and Luci's journey is filled with a wonderful insight into the Native American life. It is a love story that will fill you with warmth and contentment. You will enjoy Danny's journey to become a SEAL and his reasons for it. Good job Sharon!" (5 Star Review)

PRAISE FOR THE
BAND OF BACHELORS SERIES

"*[Lucas]* was the first book in the Band of Bachelors series and it was a phenomenal start. I loved how we got to see the other SEALs we all love and we got a look at Lucas and Marcy. They had an instant attraction, and their love was very intense. This book had it all, suspense, steamy romance, humor, everything you want in a riveting, outstanding read. I can't wait to read the next book in this series." (5 Star Review)

PRAISE FOR THE
TRUE BLUE SEALS SERIES

"Keep the tissues box nearby as you read *True Blue SEALs: Zak* by Sharon Hamilton. I imagine more than I wish to that the circumstances surrounding Zak and Amy are all too real for returning military personnel and their families. Ms. Hamilton has put us right in the middle of struggles and successes that these two high school sweethearts endure. I have read several of Sharon Hamilton's military romances but will say this is the most emotionally intense of the ones that I have read. This is a well-written, realistic story with authentic characters that will have you rooting for them and proud of those who serve to keep us safe. This is an author who writes amazing stories that you love and cry with the characters. Fans of Jessica Scott and Marliss Melton will want to add Sharon Hamilton to their list of realistic military romance writers." (5 Star Review)

"Dear FATHER IN HEAVEN,

If I may respectfully say so sometimes you are a strange God. Though you love all mankind,

It seems you have special predilections too.

You seem to love those men who can stand up alone who face impossible odds, Who challenge every bully and every tyrant ~

Those men who know the heat and loneliness of Calvary. Possibly you cherish men of this stamp because you recognize the mark of your only son in them.

Since this unique group of men known as the SEALs know Calvary and suffering, teach them now the mystery of the resurrection ~ that they are indestructible, that they will live forever because of their deep faith in you.

And when they do come to heaven, may I respectfully warn you, Dear Father, they also know how to celebrate. So please be ready for them when they insert under your pearly gates.

Bless them, their devoted Families and their Country on this glorious occasion.

We ask this through the merits of your Son, Christ Jesus the Lord, Amen."

By Reverend E.J. McMalhon S.J. LCDR, CHC, USN
Awards Ceremony SEAL Team One
1975 At NAB, Coronado